THE TEMPEST
OF
TWO LEFT
SHOES

BY

M.M BECK

Gotham Books

30 N Gould St.
Ste. 20820, Sheridan, WY 82801
https://gothambooksinc.com/

Phone: 1 (307) 464-7800

© 2023 *Milton-Beck*. All rights reserved.

No part of this book may be reproduced, stored in a retrieval system, or transmitted by any means without the written permission of the author.

Published by Gotham Books (January 6, 2023)

ISBN: 979-8-88775-182-5 (P)
ISBN: 979-8-88775-183-2 (E)

Because of the dynamic nature of the Internet, any web addresses or links contained in this book may have changed since publication and may no longer be valid.

The views expressed in this work are solely those of the author and do not necessarily reflect the views of the publisher, and the publisher hereby disclaims any responsibility for them.

INTRODUCTION

Places:
>*Cleaveland Colorado – a small town west of Colorado Rocky Mountains*
>*Knoxville, Colorado – a small city on the west slope of the Rocky Mountains, home of Knoxville College*
>
>*Fort Carson – An Army Base near Colorado Springs*
>*Peterson Field – An Air Force Base near Colorado Springs*
>*Quantico – A Maine base in Virginia, CIE headquarters*

Time:
>*October 1953*

Characters:
>*Lieutenant Colonel Daniel Jorgensen – Chief of Investigations of the Army Criminal Investigation Element (CIE)*
>*Helmut Schmidt – Manager of a ski lodge in Cleaveland, Colorado*
>*Gretta Schmidt – Wife of Helmut Schmidt*
>*Bradley Armstrong – Mayor of Cleaveland*
>*Josh Parker – Police chief of Cleaveland*
>*Grace Herndon – Police officer in Cleaveland*
>*Colonel Oakley – Army Area CIE Commander, Quantico Marine Base*
>*John March – Colorado Lieutenant Governor and friend of Dan Jorgensen*

CONTENTS

CHAPTER ONE – A PLEASANT AND PAINFUL REUNION	1
CHAPTER TWO – THE BRUTAL STORY	11
CHAPTER THREE – SO THE HUNT IS ON AGAIN	20
CHAPTER FOUR – THERE MUST NEEDS BE OPPOSITION IN ALL THINGS	27
CHAPTER FIVE - THE BIG SHOW IN COURT	35
CHAPTER SIX – CIE HEADQUARTERS	43
CHAPTER SEVEN – COME WHAT MAY	52
CHAPTER EIGHT – IS THIS THE BITTER END	60
CHAPTER NINE – A PEACEFUL LIFE	73
CHAPTER TEN – IT HAS STARTED AGAIN	81
CHAPTER ELEVEN – THE BATTLE IS JOINED	89
CHAPTER TWELVE – WHAT IS MY TASK	99
CHAPTER THIRTEEN – BACK IN THE HARNESS	105
CHAPTER FOURTEEN – ANOTHER HEAD ROLLS	117
CHAPTER FIFTEEN – THE FOX HUNT IS ON	130
CHAPTER SIXTEEN – WILL THIS EVER END	142
CHAPTER SEVENTEEN – SURPRISE MOVE	153
CHAPTER EIGHTEEN – VENGEANCE IS MINE	164
CHAPTER NINETEEN – VENGEANCE IN ACTION	175
EPILOGUE	188

CHAPTER ONE
A Pleasant and Painful Reunion

Lieutenant Colonel Dan Jorgensen arrived on Tuesday, October 20, 1953, in Cleaveland, Colorado quietly with no fanfare or notice. He was not wearing his uniform to avoid any curiosity or interest attached to himself. I hoped to see some old acquaintances and have a peaceful time away from the rat races. Such times were not found often in the Criminal Investigation Element of the Army Command. And the finding of friends was not common either. People that knew me did not like to see me coming. I hoped this would not be the case here in Cleaveland.

Dan got off the bus, looked up at the beautiful mountains and the clear blue skies. It seemed that you could see forever and the brisk clear air was almost intoxicating. Not the intoxication of alcohol but the intoxication of life. He stopped and felt something before he heard it, the whispering from the breeze in the pines on the mountain sides. It was almost like a lullaby, enough to put a person to sleep. He was thoroughly enjoying it and felt totally alive.

As Dan walked away from the bus stop dead end, for this was the end of the line. Dan looked at this once forgotten town. It had started in the late 1880s with the finding of silver and was named after President Cleveland, with a mistaken misspelled name, in hopes of attracting a rich and colorful crowd. This venture along with a limited silver vein fizzled out. The town held on by various subsistence means, mainly the water rights the town held, providing water for the farmers in the low lands. The town was quiet and not yet the center of attraction it would probably one day become.

I stopped by the local drug store, stepped in and walked to the fountain counter. The stools along the old counter and the white and black tile floors were from a distant past time. They put into me the memories of my early, carefree life and I felt at ease. I wished I could stay here forever. But that would not happen. After having an enjoyable and refreshing root beer float, like I remembered of an earlier time, I asked the young lady that served him, "Where is the ski lodge?"

She directed me, "Go two blocks east up the street and then three blocks to the north. The lodge is a large log building."

When I got close, after a brisk and pleasant walk up the mountain side, I could see the lodge. It looked a lot like a chalet of the Tyrolean Alps of my memory. It was easy to identify. The hike up to the lodge was an exhilarating exercise and the view made it even more worthwhile. The scene reminded me greatly of the Lechtal Alps to the south of Bavaria, or Bayern to the Germans. The Plansee (Plan Sea or lake) of Austria just over the mountain and border to the south of Bavaria was another scene that he remembered and enjoyed. But not the tasks I had to carry out in the town not far from there. He thought of Helmut Schmidt and the terrible events that led up to the breaking up of the criminal element that operated in the small village in the Plansee area.

Fortunately, I had been able to save Helmut from prison as Helmut had been forced to work with the gang to protect his beautiful wife Gretta. With the sub-camp of the Dachau Concentration Camp here in Plansee, Dan and Helmut could see all too well what the results would be of refusing to do the will of their evil over lords. Helmut would have wound up dead and Gretta would have been forced into prostitution. The results of the Gestapo actions in the concentration camp were hard to cover up or hide. Several mass graves could be seen around the camp. In a strongly protected and guarded workshop area was a kiln shop where a bit of gold and silver jewelry, gold teeth and silver fillings that had not been melted down and poured into bars of the heavy metals had not been processed yet. In a safe several gold bars were still there and had not been shipped to Berlin or where ever.

Dan did what he saw to be just and the best possible outcome from a terrible situation. Dan was able to obtain testimonies of witnesses in the area that Helmut had saved many local residents from capture and death. Helmut was part of an underground railway that smuggled people, that were in danger from the Gestapo, out of the country. He also had helped untold numbers of allied pilots and aircraft crew members, from planes shot down, to safe areas on their way to Switzerland. This had all helped Dan to get Helmut and Gretta to the United States.

Would Helmut be glad to see him or regret the memories his presence would bring back? What would come would come. He approached the lodge with some anxiety but moved on without hesitation. It was not in his character to avoid confronting any dreaded encounters. The quicker they were brought to the attention of the legal authorities, the quicker they were over. And often were less painful than if postponed.

With quick strides I mounted the steps to the magnificent lodge. I paused at the entrance and looked about him. The panorama was one to behold and cherish. Just a moments treasure and then into the lodge and up to the registration desk to face what may be.

The proprietor of the lodge, a burly man with gray hair and sagging shoulders turned to me and his face went suddenly pale as a ghost and then red with anger. He could hardly believe what he was seeing. The last person he wanted to confront was this criminal investigator. It brought back painful memories, memories he wished were dead and gone. The memories of the criminal band in the area of Plansee in Austria that would steal art treasures and smuggle them out for sale at high prices. They used the war as a cover for their evil work and used force and coercion to make men such as Helmut do their dirty work. But here he is, this powerful criminal investigator. Then after the initial shock of seeing again Major Jorgensen of the US Army Criminal Investigation Element (CIE), he remembered what this officer had done for him. He had kept him from going to prison and even gave support for he and Gretta to migrate to the US. Helmut, had this job because of him and decided he had to be grateful to this man even if he did bring back painful memories.

His initial fear and anger past, Helmut hurried from behind the counter and threw his large arms around this wonderful man, his benefactor. After a more agreeable greeting, he called for Gretta to come and see who was here. Gretta came out shortly, looked at Dan and her face lit up like a light bulb. She let out a joyful scream and flew into his arms. Dan stepped back, as soon as he could and looked her over. "Gretta", he said, "you are as beautiful as ever." And Gretta blushed.

Gretta was indeed a beautiful woman, she was about five feet three inches tall, honey blond hair and had startlingly blue eyes. Her figure would stop any man in his tracks. Even though she was closing in on fifty years of age, she was indeed as beautiful as ever. It is no wonder that Helmut did what he did to protect her.

Dan, Helmut and Gretta had an hour or so to bring each other up to date about their lives with pleasure. Helmut and Gretta were pleased that Dan was there on vacation rather than on business. Their lives had been more peaceful and pleasant since coming to America, but they still missed the old times from their part of Austria from before the war.

Their country was magnificent with the tall mountains of the Alps, covered with the evergreen trees. Also, the beautiful blue lake not far away and the old castle ruins on the top of the mountain. The ruins could be seen in the distance, a perfect land- mark. Helmut and Gretta had climbed to the ruins and explored them a number of times. They were interesting, yet foreboding. Why and how someone built the castle or fortress in such a place was a wonder.

Dan told them of his promotion to Lieutenant Colonel. Then he told them of his marriage, which was like one out of a story book. where they were to live happily ever after. But that was not to be. Helen was killed in a buzz bomb explosion just about three months after their marriage. Since then, he had not been able to have anything to do with women. He could not even look at a woman without the memory of Helen rising to the forefront of his memory. The memories of Helen were too painful to endure.

They discussed the mountains of Colorado being different from the Alps of Helmut and Gretta's past home. But the Colorado mountains had their grandeur as well, their magnificence and the tall pine trees. This helped to relieve their longing for home. Longing for their home land but not the history that they lived through.

Dan got a room at the lodge and went exploring the town. The town still showed some of its history as a mining town. The old tailings pile from the hard rock silver mine was still there and remnants of the old mine steeple projected up to the sky. One or two of the old saloons, the drug store and an old hotel were reminders of an exuberant past era. These along with the breathtaking scenery made the town a very picturesque sight. But the skiing and tourism were showing their impact as well. Ski shops, clothing stores and typical tourist goods suppliers were evident. Was this an improvement or not? For the business community, yes. For the rest of the people of the town, that was a big question. The new elements brought in money, for some of the town. To others, it was an intrusion in their lives. Many of the new buildings were modernistic in nature and looked sterile. They stuck out like sore thumbs and the view or sight was distasteful for many.

Dan, at thirty-five years of age, had kept in good physical shape and his military stature drew some attention from the locals as he walked about the town, especially the female populace. Dan was six foot three inches tall with light brown, wavy hair and gray eyes. He had a striking and commanding appearance. Some of the male members also noticed him with some jealousy and less than friendly attitude. This all went apparently unobserved by Dan, but he was used to it. They would all get over it when he left.

That evening Dan ate a late supper of giblet soup, a healthy slice of pumpernickel bread and a glass of apple cider. He hadn't had food like that for years and he enjoyed it. Gretta's cooking was such as a man could appreciate, and he did. Helmut was surprised that Dan still didn't drink beer or any alcohol, nor smoked. And he didn't drink coffee either. That was so different from the other American soldiers. Helmut guessed that those Mormonen were fanatics.

Tomorrow would bring another day, another wonder. I wondered what gifts of life it would bring? Morning was the beginning of another day. What is going to happen to redirect my attention and activities? I have a sixth or seventh sense that warned me of something in the air, and this morning that warning or premonition certainly seemed to fill that niche in my life. Whether I liked it or not. The itch behind my ear was working overtime and at a quick step.

The only thing that seemed out of place this morning was

the young man-eating breakfast on the other side of the dining hall. I asked Helmut about the young man. Helmut told me that the young man's name was Roy Davis, a quiet young man that didn't get into trouble. He usually stuck to himself in town or was out in the mountains being a recluse. He drew no notice to himself. It was almost as if he weren't even there. He did work for the canal company and did a good job for them.

As they quietly carried on their conversation, a man came in, looked around and made a bee line for Roy Davis. Whatever the man said to Roy, the young man didn't seem to be pleased with the message he received. Roy quickly finished his food and departed like a cat with its tail on fire.

Since the business at the lodge was a bit slow at this time of the year, Helmut and I had a casual and leisurely meal with Gretta joining us from time to time. I was glad to see them at peace with themselves and the world for the first time in years. That I had seen at least. They talked about their younger lives and what they were like before the war turned their lives into shambles. They told of their tours of the fortress of Salzburg and of the nearby salt mine. In the salt mine they wore leather aprons on their backsides. The purpose for those leather aprons worn like that was so they could sit on logs and slide down to the next level of the salt mine. In the mine there were small lakes which they would cross in small boats. I thought the sound of it was rather interesting. I had no time to see it

It was a pleasant here, but the tickle behind my ear was still letting me know something was about to happen. Whatever would likely change it all. For me at least. But what?

It wasn't long after Roy Davis had left that he was back, totally confused and seemingly disoriented. He was blubbering and making incoherent statements. Helmut and Dan were able to calm him down a bit and he said, "There is a dead woman in the canal. I didn't know what to do so I came back here to the lodge."

The lodge was the closest thing to the canal and diversion dam where he had been sent. Helmut called the deputy sheriff and the police chief. They were both on their way and they will decide whose jurisdiction this matter is. After they arrived and got what information they could drag from Roy in his excited state, Helmut again made a phone call. This time he called for the doctor to look after Roy. He certainly needed some help.

The deputy sheriff came over to me and asked who I was. I told him, "I am Lieutenant Colonel Daniel Jorgensen, Chief of Investigations of the Army Criminal Investigation Element of the Army command in Virginia." I also gave him adequate details about what I was doing here at this time, which seemed to satisfy him for the time. He asked me if I would be willing to go with them to check on the body and assist if it were needed. This was nothing new to me so it didn't bother me to assist them. The sheriff and police chief knew where the diversion dam was so it didn't take long to get there.

All of the way to the dam, they were speculating about the body being in the canal. Was the woman's body there or was it some deer or other animal's body that had somehow got caught in the canal and drowned? Was it this young man's imagination running wild? Well, it wouldn't take long to determine the truth and hope the young man was wrong. The body of a young woman would make for a lot of work and reports, besides putting a blot on the town.

The last part of the road to the canal was a dirt road. There had been some rain during the night so the road was muddy. As much of the canal was lined with clay the canal bank was slick. This didn't help matters negotiating the path along the bank of the canal. The slick clay of the canal bank would not help with the task of removing the body, if it were there. The water in the canal was brown with mud and silt picked up by the storm in the night.

The body was there all right and it didn't take a medical examination to confirm the young lady was dead. She was dressed in ski clothes and ski boots. That was strange because it was too early in the season for skiing. There was not enough snow in the mountains yet. The job of recovering the body from the canal would be tricky because of the water in the canal and the canal being lined with clay. One or two of us were going to have to get in the cold, muddy water to be able to lift the body out of the canal. I became one of the wet and muddy candidates for this aspect of the job along with the deputy sheriff.

I got the impression from watching these two officers of the law, that they were not paying much attention to details about the body. Their first concern was to get the body out of the canal. One thing I noticed was the ski mask had been turned up to expose her face. The newly exposed face had less of a film of mud than her clothes and other parts of exposed skin. Why had someone done this after the body had been put in the canal? That raised considerable concerns in my mind. As we removed her body from the canal, I noticed also, that she had two left ski boots on her feet. There was no question in my mind that this was a case of murder, but I said nothing to the officers of the law. I would pass on this information to them if needed or if they asked.

This was the jurisdiction of one or the other, not mine. Since the body was found within the limits of the town of Cleaveland, the deputy sheriff relinquished the jurisdiction in this case to the police chief. I'm not sure that Police Chief, Josh Parker, was pleased with this turn of events. This would put a strain on the time and budget of his department. This was the police chief's problem. Well, one thing at a time.

The body was transported to the morgue in the local hospital, if you could call it that. The examination would take place after the county coroner arrived. He was from the county seat thirty miles away and was expected here about one in the afternoon. It is doubtful if he would do an autopsy here in town and would take the body back to the county seat, Alder Grove, where there was a more proper facility for such.

Dan was left to himself and had to remove wet, muddy clothes and take a shower. He figured he would have these clothes laundered a bit later. After the shower he dressed in clean clothes and did his usual task at such times, he recorded all that had taken place, who was involved, time and place, and his observations. Dan always recorded all of his notes in such detail that he could answer any questioner exact details and descriptions such that the details could stand up in court. This due to his experience of testifying many times in court, as the Chief of Investigations for the local command Criminal Investigation Element (CIE). Good complete notes, recorded as quickly as possible after an event, were key to resolving questions. He was sure that there were questions to come.

And the questions came! Later that day the Police Chief came to see Dan. And he surely did ask questions. Here, Dan was a stranger in Cleaveland, and today a woman's body shows up. Who are you, what are you doing here? Who do you work for? Who is your supervisor? Was there a reason that you are here at this specific lodge? Did you already know the Schmidts? And if so, how long have you known Helmut and Gretta Schmidt? Why did you come out with us to check on the body? Dan was ready to answer the chief's questions:

1 - Who am you?
Lieutenant Colonel Daniel Jorgensen, Chief of Investigations, for the local army command Criminal Investigation Element (CIE) in Virginia.
2 - What are you doing here?
I am visiting some old friends, Helmut and Gretta Schmidt.
3 - How long have you known them?
Since before the end of World War II.
4 - Who do you work for and what do you do?
I am the Chief of Investigations and I work for the US Army Area CIE.
5 - Who is your supervisor?
Colonel Oakley, Commander of the CIE
6 - Why did you come with us to check on the body
The deputy sheriff asked me to do so after he asked me a few question to find out who I am.

It was a wonder the chief hadn't asked for my family and medical histories. Having given satisfactory answers to all of the questions, the chief settled down and contemplated me. Chief Parker asked me no questions about any observations I had made. And I did not offer any at this time. Better just wait and see the direction the wind blows and, in the meantime, keep a good record of all that happens.

The body of the young woman was found Wednesday morning; the autopsy would be performed on Thursday. The earliest that a preliminary autopsy report could be expected would be Monday or Tuesday of next week with a final report as late as the end of next month. I would like to see that report. Dan thought to himself, *I have planned to stay here a week and then I have to get back to my post. I will probably receive a subpoena and have to come back, but that can be arranged. I had better notify the Colonel about what has happened so all of this won't take him off guard.*

Roy Davis had been put into a hospital or clinic in Alder Grove, with a make shift psychiatric ward. This was at the county seat where they could help him overcome the trauma of finding the body. He was having terrible nightmares and he was certainly not sleeping very well. That was too bad to happen to such a young man. Who knows what the rest of his life would be like. And I wondered about all of the young men drafted into the military that had to kill people. How do they cope with such in their minds?

CHAPTER TWO
The Brutal Story

Dan was eating a small supper at the lodge, eating slowly and enjoyed the background music, Strauss waltzes. As he was close to being finished, the police chief came in and approached him at his table and asked, "May I sit down?"

Dan replied "Be my guest."

Chief Parker sat and looked at Dan for a time before speaking, then he said "I checked you out and found that you have some reputation in the military as an investigator. I was told by your commander that you have a knack at seeing things that others don't and can piece together puzzles that leave almost everyone else confused. Would you mind telling me what you have made out of this situation I have on my hands, about the body of the young lady we pulled from the canal?"

Dan pondered the request for a moment, then replied to the chief's query. "I would be glad to tell you anything I know and even what I suspect or believe about this case. I have made notes of my observations and thoughts from the beginning of my involvement. It would be best if I could review my notes before telling you anything. I don't want to give any misleading ideas by telling you everything based on just my current memory. Would it be alright if I meet with you in the morning, or do you want to meet with me in a half an hour at your office?"

"Let us meet in my office in thirty minutes then, and thanks." Chief Parker arose, nodded his head and left the lodge.

Well, Dan thought, that was quite a change of attitude. Dan finished his meal and went to his room, wondering about the chief's change toward him. The thought came to mind, *You don't suppose the name of my friend came up and the chief contacted him. It doesn't hurt to have friends in high places, like John March being the Lieutenant Governor of this state. Well, if so then my position here is standing on a little more firm foundation than it would have been otherwise.*

The time for his meeting with the chief was drawing closer

and he picked up his notes and quickly scanned them. He glanced out the window as he heard the howl of a gust of wind. Snow was beginning to fall and it looked like it was going to be a cold night, and not a pleasant walk to the chief's office and back. Going down stairs he encountered Helmut who looked at him in surprise. "You are going out at this time and in this weather?"

"I'm going down to see the Police Chief like he asked me and he has some questions for me," said Dan.

Helmut offered, "Let me drive you down. It is bitter outside now."

"Thanks", said Dan, "I'll take you up on that. I do not relish that walk just now with that wind and blowing snow. What is the Chief like?" asked Dan on the drive down town.

Helmut told Dan, "He seems to be a decent police officer. He does not push his weight around and seems to treat people fairly, that is unless his son and the son of the mayor are involved. Then any complaints or charges are swept under the carpet and forgotten. By the local authorities at least."

Dan hoped that those two were not involved with this murder, or more correctly, with this double murder. Of this bit of information Dan was sure, based on his observations. The one question he had was, *Where is the body of the other girl?*

When Dan arrived at the police office, he got out and thanked Helmut for the ride and information. He looked at the one story, older and unimpressive cement block building that housed the police department. It certainly looked a bit decrepit next to the city hall. The police department building could at least use a fresh coat of paint, preferably something other than morgue gray. The city hall on the other hand had all of the adornments possible to make it look bright and impressive. This told Dan a fair amount regarding the politics of the city of Cleaveland, Colorado.

Dan entered gladly to get out of the bitter wind and was shown to the chief's office by a rather attractive young female uniformed officer. Her uniform didn't leave much to the imagination and she blushed when Dan looked at her. At least all of the trimmings of this office weren't taken up by the mayor. Maybe the mayor just hadn't paid much attention to the police department. *Who knows, but the Shadow isn't here.* Dan thought and wondered about that, how many people now days know or remember anything about the radio program of *The Shadow,* what with the television now so popular?

Chief Parker asked Dan to sit. The young officer came in also with a steno pad to record everything he said. Her gaze at Dan did not apparently seem entirely professional. The chief noticed me looking his officer over and smiled. He introduced the officer as Grace Herndon, smiling. And the chief suddenly had a twinkle in his eye.

Dan wondered if the information the chief had received about himself included that about his wife. His wife that had been killed in England during one of the buzz bomb raids and explosions. Dan was a long time recovering from her untimely death and could not so much as look at a woman since. Why now? It had been a little over eight years since the death of his wife. It had hit him hard and he had put his whole attention and efforts into his work as an investigator. But there was something about this young lady that caught Dan's attention like a big magnet. He had encountered some beautiful women in his life but they didn't attract or affect him any more than water on a duck's back. This startled Dan a bit; however, he had learned not to show any emotions. This characteristic was of great value in his line of work.

Dan quickly put his mind to the task at hand and cleared it. He pulled out his notes and began to organize his thoughts so as to present this information in the most coherent manner. He began his statement by describing some of the details of his observations of the woman's body. The two left ski boots on her feet. The fact that the ski mask had been turned up some time after being placed or thrown into the canal. This later detail would not have been apparent had there not been the rain storm that muddied the water in the canal. This brought up a question to his mind, *Why did the killer, or killers come back and make this change? That change would draw more attention to this being a murder case, unless the guilty party or parties didn't expect the body to be found so soon.*

The longer the body was in the canal, the less attention would have been made to that change.

Dan's conclusions: derived at by putting two and two together were as follows:

The girl, or young woman had been probably sexually involved or molested.

Then she was murdered or unintentionally smothered to quiet her.

There was also another girl involved, one about the same size as the one whose body was found. This based on shoe sizes and two left shoes being on the body.

The second girl was also probably dead.

One of the two girls was probably killed accidentally and the second was murdered to quiet her and cover up the crime.

There were two or more men involved with this crime. Probably.

Three Recommendations:

The shoes of the girl must be examined and her body checked for sexual involvement. Hopefully the coroner has already done the latter.

A check with missing persons might produce an identity of the young woman whose body was found. Also, it might lead to a second missing young woman and start a search for her body.

Have you already been considering looking for two young men of questionable character and questioning them?

After this last statement, Dan noticed the startled look on the face of the young female officer that was recording his statement. Dan did not react to her change in appearance but kept looking at the chief's face. The chief's face was suddenly stern and hard, then just as suddenly expressionless. Dan was sure the chief hoped his facial changes had not been seen. This was of importance to Dan. What does this mean? He was sure he would know about that shortly whether they liked it or not. Dan finished his statement and then asked Chief Parker, "Could I see the shoes the girl was wearing?"

The chief said, "They were probably over to the county seat. Tomorrow Officer Herndon could drive you over to the coroner's office ".

Dan agreed with that and left the police station. The snow and wind were worse now than when he came down. He was starting to walk in the direction of the lodge when Officer Herndon came out and offered him a ride, which he gladly accepted. He accepted for more than just a ride to the lodge in this weather. He wanted a chance to be with and talk with Miss Herndon. Miss because she did not have a ring on her left hand. Neither hand for that matter. The ride to the lodge gave Dan the chance to talk with Grace Herndon and he asked her about her response when he mentioned that two young men were probably involved. She replied that she would rather not say just now, but tomorrow she would probably tell him. She dropped him off at the lodge and quickly left. Dan would have liked to talk to her more, and not about the case either.

Tomorrow would give him a chance. Also, while they were at the county seat, he would like to see Roy Davis to see how he was doing. Roy had a hard shock at finding the dead young lady in the canal. Dan wondered if the canal had been shut off, since that was probably what Roy had been sent to do.

That night Dan didn't sleep much nor very well. The scene where the body was found and the reactions of the police chief and officer Herndon when Dan had mentioned two young men of questionable character kept coming into his mind. And the image of Grace Herndon seemed to pop into his mind all on its own. She was a rather petite young lady, but the look of her arms indicated that she could do a favorable job at protecting herself considering the bulge of her upper arms. She was brunette, Gray eyes with a touch of green. Her eyes probably will appear differently depending on source, intensity, and type of light. She had a clear and slightly tan complexion. She didn't wear cosmetics, she didn't have to. To Dan she was his Venus. At least he was beginning to hope so.

Dawn came sooner than Dan would have liked because he hadn't slept much. But he had never known how to stop a clock or stop the earth from turning. Dawn it was. He hurriedly got ready and dressed for breakfast and went down to the dining room. Officer Herndon was there having a continental breakfast while she waited for him. Dan wondered what her attitude was this morning. Would she be willing to talk with him or clam up cold?

Dan joined her and enjoyed the breakfast served, enjoyed

it because the food was good, but even more since Officer Herndon was there with him. Dan always enjoyed the food he got used to in Europe and Gretta was a good cook. They had small talk over their meal but Officer Herndon was standoffish and really appeared like she didn't want to talk. She seemed as if she would like to get this drive over with as quickly as possible.

Their meals finished, they proceeded out to the patrol car and left for the county seat, Alder Grove, some thirty miles away. The roads were snow covered so this was not going to be a speedy drive. That was fine as far as Dan was concerned. He had reason to be with Officer Herndon beyond that of just his questions pertaining to this murder case. Dan didn't force a conversation nor push the issue of her reaction about the mention of the two young men that Dan had suggested should be questioned. Dan asked a couple of questions about her and she answered them civilly. After a time, she even began to open up a bit and relax. He hoped she was not afraid of him or intimidated.

Dan also wondered about his attraction to Grace Herndon. He had never experienced such an attraction since the death of his wife. Dan didn't like to think even about his wife's name because it was so painful even now, eight years since her death in England. Another death caused by a buzz bomb.

They arrived in Alder Grove and she took him to the morgue. The coroner was in his office and had been waiting for them, after the police chief had called him and told him of Dan's request. The coroner took them to the room where personal effects were stored, the room was not locked. They entered and the coroner opened the locker where the clothes of the deceased young woman were being held. He searched through them and stopped. He looked puzzled and turned to Dan. "Her shoes are gone ". The room was not locked and the lockers were not locked unless there were valuables involved. Who would want her ski boots?

Dan asked the coroner, "Did you notice anything about the boots?" He didn't ask any leading questions such as, "Were both ski boots for the left feet?" Dan didn't want to alter the coroner's memory which leading questions can do. Dan's question shook up the coroner, especially since he had not noticed anything about the boots. This was not something to overlook, especially in a murder case...

The loss of the ski boots struck Dan as a critical issue in this case. Whoever took them had inside information and also had access to this facility. How many people fit into this category? Did the young men fit? Chalk up one more inquiry to make. Dan and Officer Herndon left the morgue and went to the clinic where Roy Davis was being treated. They were allowed to see and talk with him. Roy seemed to be handling the situation quite well.

They returned to the patrol car and headed back to Cleaveland. Their conversations this time were more open and freer. Dan found out that she was not married and had no real prospects. She was twenty-seven years old, had one sister and three brothers. She was the oldest child in her family. She seemed to come out of her shell a bit more. But she still wouldn't tell him why she reacted as she did at the mention of two young men.

By the time they got back to Cleaveland, Dan asked her for a date. She hesitated, but in the end agreed. She would meet him at the lodge for an evening dinner day after tomorrow. He had made some progress and felt more enthusiastic by the time she pulled up in front of the lodge. Dan thanked her and got out of the patrol car. She leaned over toward the open door and looked up into his face with tears in her eyes. She held out her hand and took his and apologized for not being able to tell him about the two young men. She also said that she was looking forward to their dinner. Dan stepped back, closed the door and she was off. He was now a bit depressed, seeing her drive away. Why?

He would have to watch how his mixed emotions affected him. He felt sure the word would get out, and it always did, about his ideas concerning the murders. Would they try for him? He fully expected them to try sooner or later. This was not a new game. He had played this game many times over the years as an investigator for Army CIE where he worked.

Dan went into the dining hall for lunch and noticed the latest local newspaper lying on one of the tables. He picked it up expecting to read the typical small-town news. That was not what he found. Instead, there in bold large print were the headlines, **MURDERED WOMAN FOUND IN CLEAVELAND.** The rest of the article included much of his observations and conclusions. Someone had wasted no time in passing his statement to the press. The newspaper must have stopped the presses to make this story front page so soon, overnight.

Well, this would put him square in the "burn the witch" hunt, or rather in this case, "burn the wizard" hunt. If the two young men were locals, he would have to watch his back even more because he was sure they would "try" for him. The question was, "When?". "Where?"

Helmut came over and joined him. He glanced at the headlines and said, "It looks like old times again." Old times is right. Dan had spent much of his life looking for the scum of the earth with one hand on his 45 and an eye to his rear. That is where they usually came at him from. The rough element had come close at least a couple of times. He hoped this wouldn't be the one where they succeeded. Now that it seemed, that he might have something to live for.

Gretta joined them and peered into Dan's eyes and smiled. "Well, is she the one?" Gretta didn't waste time beating around the bush.

Dan told her, "I don't know, but I kind of hope so. I haven't felt like this since...."

Gretta then told him "She is a beautiful and very good girl. You would have to look for one or two lives to find anyone better".

Dan hoped that he wouldn't have to have one or two lives to find out if she were the one. So much for love and war. He had certainly walked into it this time. He would have to be even more alert than ever before. At least he had a reason to be so and hoped that he was up to it. After his lunch he walked up to the canal to look the site over. Luckily, he had been able to acquire a good pair of boots. The snow would have made the walk an unpleasant one without them. The hike of about one half of a mile to the canal through six inches of snow was not what a person would really want. The scene on the other hand was that of a winter wonderland. One to enjoy.

He was standing on the canal back looking it over when his foot slipped out from under him. While he was trying to regain a stable footing again, the report of rifle fire caught up and the whizzing he had heard as he fell made sense. Evidently the guilty had not hesitated any time at all to eliminate him. They were keeping an eye on him. And rifles were common in this area. He ducked and slid down into the empty canal for protection. He followed the canal for about three hundred yards which took him around a bend.

There he found some trees close to the canal that blocked the view from the direction the bullet had come. He used a low hanging branch to pull himself out of the canal. He had to find a path back to the lodge, one that would give him cover. He found one in a few minutes. It was not exactly what he wanted but it wasn't bad. The hike back to the lodge a bit slower. He did not use the path of his trek to the canal and he made sudden turns in order to not present a good target for a second try at his life. This would make them more cautious and more dangerous also. At least he made it back to the lodge without drawing more gun fire.

Should he report this to Chief Parker. All things considered he didn't think that would be a good idea. His statement to the chief had been in the paper the next day. Was the chief the source of the that? Did he give the information to the newspaper? And he did not want Grace Herndon to hear about it either. He would just have to enter this in his log and carry it with him. He wondered how secure his room was. What would they try next time? They knew this land and therefore had an advantage in that aspect of the cat and mouse game. But they probably did not have his experience in this deadly game of hide and seek.

When Dan got back to the lodge, he looked for Helmut for a conversation and information about the younger male population of the town. He found Helmut but he was busy at the time. Helmut agreed to talk with Dan later.

CHAPTER THREE
So, The Hunt is on Again

Dan walked down to town and found the public library. He went in and inquired about their collection of local newspapers. Dan found the stack of past publications of the newspapers. He began doing a cursory review of them. The seventh issue he came across had an article about two young men that had an altercation with some youth of another town. They were Paul Armstrong; son of the mayor, and Will Parker, the son of the police chief of Cleaveland. This was interesting. Further review of the old papers brought up the names of these two a number of times, not always dealing with troubles, but also showing them to be the heroes of the town. So, heroes and trouble makers, the big sports kings of the community. And the sons of the two most influential men of the town. Might this be the answer he was seeking? It certainly gave him a target for investigation. It also fit into the picture that he remembered about the reaction of Chief Parker and Officer Herndon when he mentioned two young men. That would be a good place to start in the murder investigation. Things seem to be fitting into place.

Dan knew that just because this fit the picture, he must not put other possibilities aside and forgotten. The only thing is that there were currently no other possible pieces to the puzzle, at this time. As Dan went back to the lodge, taking note of who he saw on the street, what cars drove the town and if any of the cars were seen repeatedly. Some possibilities showed up and when he got back to his room, he would make note of his sightings along with the newspaper information.

When Dan got to the lodge and went in, he saw a rather beefy man standing at the reception counter, speaking loudly and gesticulating vigorously with his hands. Dan heard part of what he was saying, that he wanted to take apart this incompetent blow hard that has come here causing problems for my town and my son. Helmut pointed to me and the beefy loud mouth turned around to me, his face almost as red as a garden beet. I figured he better calm down or he would talk himself into a heart attack.

The big man plunged toward me with his fists balled up and snorting like a raging bull. He swung his fist at me and I calmly stood there and slapped his fist aside. He swung again and I just ducked to the side and he fell forward off balance and landed on his face. He got up and said, "So. You're a smart-alack too. I'll show you; you can't slander my son and get away with it. I'll have you picking cotton in the rain ".

I replied, "Who is this son of yours that I have slandered? And who are you that you can shove people around like you were the king of the manure pile and get away with it?"

This infuriated the overweight bully even more. He yelled, "I'll show you who I am. I own this town and I run it as well. I'm the mayor and I'll have you arrested within the hour."

Again, I answered his raving and said, "You and who else's army will arrest me? I have not broken any law. I have not slandered anyone and I would recommend that you calm down before you kill yourself and consider apologizing to me, Lieutenant Colonel Dan Jorgensen of the Criminal Investigation Element of the US Army."

The beefy man looked a bit taken back, turned and stormed out of the lodge. Helmut apologized for the incident and told me he was the mayor of this town. He thinks he's a big man, but he is really a small fry in a little pond.

After supper of some of his favorite German food, Helmut found him and sat down at his table with him. Since there were no other patrons nearby, Dan began his inquiry about the young crowd of the town. The information he gathered from Helmut about the two young men being somewhat of trouble makers just about totally copied what he had gathered from the newspapers. Another item was that Paul Armstrong, the son of the beefy blowhard Dan encountered when he entered the lodge a short while ago, was a two-bit Romeo and the heart throb of the girls in town. The girls of the town, they were enjoying being in love, or infatuated, with Paul. Had they married him they would have learned that it was hell to be married to him. They never learn until it's too late.

One added piece of information Helmut supplied was that

the sons mentioned were avid hunters with quite an array of rifles and prided themselves as expert marksmen. Then Dan described the cars he noted on his return to the lodge. One of them, a fancy sports car, belonged to Paul Armstrong; the son of the mayor. Interesting indeed. The pieces of the puzzle he was working on might actually be the only pieces to finally fit the puzzle.

According to Ockham's razor, *among competing hypotheses, the one with the fewest assumptions should be selected.* William of Ockham (c.1287–1347) was an English Franciscan friar, scholastic philosopher and theologian that put together this method of problem solving. The current hypothesis or theory, the only one he had at this time, seemed to have few assumptions. Perhaps it is correct. Another interpretation is that the simplest of two or more competing theories is preferred. In any case this one need full attention.

That night Dan didn't sleep much better than the night before. His mind was busy sorting out all of the information, cataloging it. The more he worked the information over, the tighter the fit of his theory. With one possible attempt on his life, he had no doubts that others would follow. Would there be another attempt by rifle? That was a possibility, but rifle bullets are easy to trace. Unless the bullets were cast entirely of lead. I wonder if either of these two young men reloaded his own shells? That shouldn't be too difficult to check out. If so, another attempt by rifle was more likely. That is if one or both of them were acquainted with ballistics. The son of the police chief might be a good candidate along this line of thought.

Friday morning, and someone kept popping up in his mind, Grace Herndon. And he wondered what were her feelings about him. If hers were anything like his, this relationship (if it could be called that) could not go on for long separately. Dan only hoped that her feelings were close to those of his own. This evening was a long time away. Too long for comfort. He also wondered what to wear for dinner. He considered wearing his dress uniform with all of the fruit salad (ribbons and awards) as well. He would decide that a bit later.

Dan, after breakfast, went for a walk through the woods using a trail Helmut had told him about. This time he took his

Colt 45 with him just in case. He walked at a leisurely pace for some time, stopping to check every now and then to listen for the sounds to see if someone might be following him. Occasionally he heard what could have been someone, but he could not be sure. At last, he came to a spot that offered a place where he could stop and observe his possible stalkers and be blocked from their view. He waited a few minutes and finally two men came along, apparently following his tracks. Both were armed with hunting rifles and wore ski masks. When they got close, Dan told them, 'Stop and drop your guns." They both turned quickly towards the sound of his voice and fired. They came close but Dan fired and hit one in the arm. He had not attempted to hit a vital organ, only to stop them. The one not hit began to fire his semiautomatic rifle in his general direction.

Dan had dropped to the ground and fired at the man still holding his rifle. Dan backed off and left the area without them trying to follow him. Score one for me. That ought to slow them down. He wondered who had been wounded. Dan made it back to the lodge, cleaned and reloaded his pistol. Then he began to clean up and change clothes. No use to alarm anyone. Let those two thinks this over and realize he was no push over.

Dan spent the remainder of the morning reading a book that he had brought with him, *Les Misérables.* The book was one of his favorites. It was by Victor Hugo, a great author. One of his favorite quotes from that book was, "*the civilized world, in every part of the globe, fires off daily one hundred and fifty thousand useless canon shots. At six francs per shot, that amounts to nine hundred thousand francs a day, or three hundred million a year, gone up in smoke.* This is only one item. Meanwhile, the poor are dying of hunger."

Victor Hugo had seen this and worked to establish peace for his people, even though they had banished him from his own home. Can't we have peace?

Come lunch time, Dan was as anxious and nervous as the proverbial cat on a hot tin roof. What was he going to do tonight? What was he going to wear? As nervous as he was the worst thing, he could do was show himself in public. In a public that probably had a couple of fearful, angry, tensed up young men that wanted him dead. But to stay here cooped up was almost as unbearable.

His training had prepared him for the worst, but how could it be worse than this?

He went down for lunch but could only eat a meager meal, during which he had pleasant conversation with Helmut and a short one with Gretta. Most of the time she was there, she kept looking at Dan out of the corners of her eyes, with a knowing smile on her face. Dan wasn't fooling her a bit... He was acting like a teenager going out on his first date. This basically was his first date. The first date in his new life, because that is what it was. He was antsy and couldn't sit still. If he got up, he would apparently walk aimlessly with no sense of a goal or task to finish. If there were a destination to his meandering, it would not be obvious to anyone else.

Now, he had to keep his mind on this murder case. He had to outsmart those young men that acted out of lust. Acted out of animal instinct and put themselves into a situation where their lives would never be the same again. Even if they get away today, or tomorrow, they will always be looking over their shoulders wondering when the long arm of the law was going to sneak up on them. They probably knew he was one of the long arms. From their actions he figured they believed that he had them pegged. The only way to defeat me was to stop me permanently. Preferably with a bullet between the eyes. So far, he had escaped them and evaded them a couple of times. How many more attempts would they need? Maybe they could run him down. A hit and run. Just an accident. They had to find an old car that they could borrow, without the owner's knowledge of course. Then watch him as he walked the streets. They would get their chance and then *wham*. It would be all over and they would be safe.

A murder to cover up a murder. Would it ever end? If only they knew what Dan Jorgensen knew. The only ones that got away were those that faced up to their crime and paid the price demanded by society. Then when it was over, they could breathe free. To a point. Their conscience would always be with them telling them what they had done. Would they ever be free? Dan was reading what newspapers he could find or order. Surely someone would find the other girl and a piece of the puzzle could be put in place. Then a predator could be put away. Put away from society and make society a little safer. Dan found no information to provide that piece of the puzzle. After lunch Dan went up to his room and entered.

Something wasn't right in the room. There was something out of place. Then he noticed the pillow. He got a broom and carefully lifted up a corner of the pillow. There was an object under it. Dan was no explosive ordinance expert, but he usually recognized one when he saw one. He called Helmut and asked him if there was a bomb squad anywhere in the area. There was not, so Dan asked Helmut to evacuate the immediate area of the lodge.

Dan called his commander and asked him to get a bomb person on the line for him. Dan would describe the bomb to the ordinance person and have the ordinance man tell Dan how to defuse the bomb. The bomb squad commander and his master sergeant, who was a top bomb expert, were quickly on the line with him

The process went slowly, but Dan was able to defuse the bomb safely, one step at a time, in about one hour. This was a tricky job and Dan was about as nervous as he was relative to his date this evening. Dan wondered if his shaking hands would cause the bomb to blow up. All during the process of working on the bomb, following the instructions of the bomb expert, Dan was sweating and shaking. He was about as nervous as a young lady playing a piano concerto as a solo for the first time before a large audience. But he had finally defused the bomb. Now he could take a deep sigh of relief. The deputy sheriff showed up and carried the bomb away for disposal. The police chief had not been told about the bomb as Dan did not want Officer Herndon to know about it. But how do you keep something like this quiet?

By the time this was all over, Dan was able to calm down. He had to face the more terrifying situation, his first date. Dan was at last able to prepare for his date. He decided that there was no reason to hide what he was so he got out his dress uniform and got it ready, fruit salad and all. After the profuse sweating while defusing the bomb, Dan was in need of a good shower. After his shower and when he was completely dressed and ready, he looked at himself in the mirror and decided that he might be considered a bit impressive looking and he hoped Grace thought so too. Well, it was time to go down stairs and meet her for their dinner.

He walked down stairs and there were a number of people in the foyer and they turned and looked up at him, almost in shock. Grace walked in, and she looked beautiful. Her jaw dropped open when she saw him and Dan smiled. To Dan, she was the only person in the foyer, despite the buzz of conversation and gasps of their audience. Dan walked to her and took her hand in his and led her to the dining room. The Schmidts had prepared a table specifically for them. They did make quite a spectacle, and a fancy one at that.

Dan may have been very nervous but Grace seemed as calm as a cool summer breeze. Her eyes seemed to be able to see no one other than Dan. She had a smile on her face and when they began to talk, she talked with him as if she had known him for years. She was calm and a pleasant conversationalist.

The food that Gretta had prepared for them was tremendous, but I noticed none of it. Talking with Grace was the only thing in my life. I hoped Grace felt the same way about me that I felt about her. When we finished our meal, I stood up and took her hand and led her out onto the dance floor. Another Strauss waltz was being played. Our dancing was spectacular and had the attention of all those in the dining hall, and even a few from out in the foyer that were standing in the doorway watching them.

I didn't need to talk, being with Grace was enough for me. At first when we started dancing, Grace danced almost at arm's length. Then she came closer and finally was dancing with my arms around her. That is where she belonged.

CHAPTER FOUR
There Must Needs Be Opposition in All Things

There Must Needs Be Opposition in All Things. Grace was certainly the opposite of the attempts made on my life. The attempts on my life were to snuff it out. Grace on the other hand brought me to life, she was my life. After the dancing, I led Grace out of the dining hall and into another room for privacy. I took Grace in my arms and kissed her. She kissed me back. It turned out that Grace evidently felt much the same for me as I felt for her.

Conversation wasn't necessary to communicate this. our being together was pure bliss.

Grace finally sat down on a couch with Dan and asked him about the bomb. Dan told her about it as briefly as possible without leaving any critical details out. Grace leaned back and looked him over and said "You are impressive. How come you didn't tell me about yourself and your rank?"

Dan's reply was simple, "The rank doesn't determine what or who I am, but I decided that you needed to know. I am the Chief of Investigations at the Criminal Investigation Element of our command."

That night Dan didn't sleep much again, but this time for a different reason. He didn't have to worry about how Grace felt about him. He was alive and enjoying it.

Saturday started uneventfully. After lunch Grace showed up and that was an event of a life time. They just sat around and talked by the hour. She asked Dan about his military career and seemed impressed with what he had gone through. She asked him what his wife was like. Somehow that was not as painful to discuss it with her as he had expected. Grace was easy to talk with.

Dan then asked Grace about her life. She said, "Most of my life has been right here in Cleaveland. I worked in the grocery store after high school. I took a correspondence class for stenography and passed with pretty good grades. That is what opened the door to the police department. My training with the police department was all on the job. I figured that was where I would stay. There was no one here that interested me. That is until you showed up and I was swept off my feet, I didn't know what to do."

They had a wonderful end to a remarkable day.

Sunday was something else. Grace had asked me if I would go to church with her. The church was in Alder Grove, so she would pick me up in her car. She had asked me to wear my uniform like I had for our date. The ride to Alder Grove was far different than the one in her patrol car.

When he got to the church it only took one look to know what church she belonged to. Life was wonderful and this was no coincidence. Dan got to meet her family. Then he got another surprise, her father was the bishop.

The bishop asked for a few minutes of Dan's time. They went into his office. Dan told him about his first wife and her death. Dan told him, "I could never even look at a woman since the death of my wife. That is until I met Grace. Then I was hit over the head with a baseball bat. We are perfectly happy together and now Grace is my life. I hope to get a job at a college in the area in the near future. Then we can live close to here where she can see you and the rest of the family. "

The bishop asked, "So you plan to get married?"

Dan's reply was, "Yes, we plan to do that as soon as possible. We would like to be married in the temple. But that will take some time so, we will probably be married civilly at first and then be sealed as soon as we can."

"That was a fast courtship, wasn't it? Are you a member of this church?" Bishop Herndon asked.

Dan said, "Yes, I have been a member all of my life. As for fast, it seems to have gone as slow as cold molasses. I don't want to be separated from Grace at all, or ever, if I have anything to say about it ".

Monday morning, 26 October., Dan walked down to the police station to talk with the chief. He went by a rather meandering route so as to provide as little of a target as possible. When he got there the first person he saw was Grace. At first her face glowed for a second and then grave concern took over. "This is dangerous to walk down here. Call and I will come and get you. I don't want to lose you", she said. Dan assured her that he would accept her offer here after. She showed him into the chief's office and left.

The chief wanted to know all about the bomb incident, which didn't take too long. Dan explained, "I called my CIE Commander and asked for a bomb disposal expert so he could talk me through the defusing of this bomb. It was a real nerve-racking hour and when the bomb was defused, the deputy sheriff took it away for disposal ".

Dan then asked the chief, "Are there any preliminary results on the autopsy?"

He said, "She had sexual contact and she had died of strangulation. There was also evidence that she had put up a fight. She had skin or flesh particles under her finger nails and bruised knuckles:

The chief then asked Dan about his idea of two murders and there being two young men involved. This took some time to explain. Chief Parker did not seem pleased with Dan's explanation for there being two murderers and two murders, but he gave no argument against his ideas.

The chief then asked, "Do you by chance happen to suspect my son in this case?"

Dan paused a bit and told the Police Chief, "I'm afraid I do, along with the son of your mayor. If I were to guess, I would say that the real perpetrator in this case was Paul Armstrong and your son was probably roped in by Paul. I have no evidence to prove my idea but the circumstantial evidence is mounting. Does your son do any loading of rifle ammunition?"

Chief Parker said, "Yes and I believe that Paul does too. Why?"

Dan answered the Chief's question, "The bomb attempt on my life wasn't the first one. The day that my conclusions and observations showed up in the newspaper, a rifle shot just missed me when my foot slipped and I nearly fell. I seem to be living on luck alone ".

"Would I be asking too much if I asked you to leave town and let this settle down a bit?" the Chief asked.

"No." Dan said, "In fact I am planning to leave shortly. I must warn you though, when I leave you will lose a nice-looking police officer. We plan to be married."

Chief Parker commented, "That was quick. You don't waste time. Well good luck. This really doesn't surprise me. I noticed how you both looked at one another that first time when you met. Love at first sight would be my guess."

"You're right." Dan said.

When Dan was ready to go, Grace was out on a call, so Dan started to walk back to the lodge. It was a cold but pleasant day for all that. He walked up the road east and started to cross the road to go north, paused and looked in all directions and it looked clear. He proceeded to cross the road and an old pickup came careening around the corner. Dan jumped to the side so the truck missed him by a matter of inches. He noticed only that there were no visible license plates on the old Chevy truck. Well, one more try. Does that mean that if he had nine lives like a cat, that the number of his lives was dwindling rather fast? Better not let Grace hear about this one.

Dan went on to the lodge where he called his commander and told him of the situation. The Colonel stated, "I want you to return to the post immediately and arrangements would be made for you to return to Cleaveland with a bodyguard. You are too valuable to us."

Dan called Grace and told her he had to return to the post immediately. She wasn't surprised but wasn't happy about it either. Dan asked her if she would go with him. She paused for a moment and asked that they talk with Dad before anything concrete was decided. Grace picked him up in her car and they drove to the business where her father worked. He agreed for Grace to go with him if they were married. They had no problem with this. They then drove to the court house and purchased a marriage license. They were married by her father that day, 26 October 1953. And both radiated with happiness.

They left the next day and stopped at a jewelry store in Alder Grove and Dan bought a diamond engagement ring and a wedding ring of Grace's choice and a wedding band for himself. They ought to do things right. They then drove to Denver and caught a plane to Washington National, just outside of Washington DC. where Dan rented a car. They drove to the command CIE headquarters on the Quantico marine base…

Dan reported to the Colonel and introduced his wife. This surprised the Colonel greatly because he knew that Dan would not even look at a woman. This was a concern since this made Dan more vulnerable and this compromised his position in the CIE. Dan would have to be kept at the headquarters here after. Dan was given verbal orders, which would be issued on paper the next day, and Dan was dismissed. Dan took Grace to his quarters. Then he told Grace, "This is some honeymoon."

She replied, "Its fine, I'm with you."

Wednesday, Dan was able to take care of a few things in the office and then arranged for them to go back to Colorado to finish up there. Dan had already been able to tell Grace about his first wife and her death. She was amazed that he had been unable to look at a woman since her death. She fully understood his feeling about her as she experienced the same feelings about him. Their marriage was truly special. And they both felt it. Dan's enlistment was up soon and Dan figured he would get out so he and Grace could be together more than this job would allow. It would also be ten years sooner than he had planned.

He could go back to veterinary work. He hadn't lost all of that. On the other hand, maybe he could get a job at some college and teach. He thought, "I definitely know quite a bit about law enforcement and history. I am well qualified in martial arts. With some refresher I could teach biology. I'm not down and out. I could even teach ROTC and retain my status as an active-duty officer and build up my retirement."

Thursday, Dan finished at the CIE offices that which he needed to do and they departed for Colorado and Cleaveland. They drove back to the Washington National Airport and took the first flight out to Denver. In Denver they picked up Grace's car and headed for Cleaveland their next stop was Cleaveland, aside from a stop or two for gas and food along the way.

They drove to the lodge and went in to register. There were two police officers there in the lodge, obviously waiting for Dan, judging by their behavior when he entered. They served Dan with a warrant for his arrest, hand cuffed him and began to escort him out of the building. As Dan was being taken out, he called to Grace, "Call my office ".

Not a pleasant end to a good day with us, together. Grace called the CIE office and told the officer on duty what had happened. Then Grace went and talked with Helmut and Gretta. Helmut told her to call the Lieutenant Governor who was one of Dan's friends. That would have to wait till tomorrow however.

The next morning Grace received a call from the Colonel. He was furious and told her, "I will have ten of my best operatives in Cleaveland before the day is out. They will be uniformed and armed. I will also send two good lawyers from the office of the Judge Advocate General's office out there. Those people there won't know what hit them".

Grace then called the office of the Lieutenant Governor and was able to talk with him. He said he would clear his calendar and be there by the end of the day. He wasn't going to abandon a friend that saved his life if there were anything he could do. He would also bring a deputy attorney general and the commander of the National Guard, a General, with him.

Grace went down to the police office and asked to see Dan. They were reluctant to let her in to see him, but she was finally allowed in. She could only reach through the bars and there was a police officer present all of the time. Grace was able to whisper to him, "The cavalry is on its way in full force." Dan was tickled. "Let's see how they handle this ".

The first to arrive was a contingent of CIE personnel with one lawyer. The police chief didn't want them to see Dan but the lawyer presented him with orders issued by a federal judge. The chief couldn't ignore that. Unhappily he allowed the lawyer and one CIE person in to see Dan. The lawyer insisted in meeting with Dan in private. Again, the chief was forced to allow it. The lawyer was able to get a pretty complete account of the story from Dan. They then left but left two CIE officers at the station with orders to see that Dan was protected and treated fairly.

The next to arrive was the Lieutenant Governor along with the deputy attorney general and the General over the National Guard. The General had even brought along four National Guard men, one officer, a captain, and three enlisted personnel, all armed. Then the remainder of the CIE personnel arrived along with the last lawyer from the Judge Advocate General's office. A female with the rank of Lieutenant Colonel.

Chief Parker, about this time was really wondering what he had bitten into. The deputy sheriff was sitting back and watched with a slight smile on his face. The mayor was present and he was beside himself, "This whole fiasco is likely to blow up in my face. The police chief and I are going to be lucky if we are still in office by the end of the week ".

The entire issue had attracted every news reporter within 500 miles of Cleaveland. No one could find a room in which to stay, within 60 miles of the town. There was so much fuss that the county judge from Alder Grove decided that a hearing must take place quickly and the best place to hold it was in Cleaveland. That wasn't necessarily to his liking but this seemed to be the best solution under the circumstances. Well, the publicity could give him good coverage. This wouldn't hurt him in the election next year. Especially if the popular feeling of the people were accorded their preferred verdict. The problem was that the opinion of the people wasn't known at this time. Time would tell. He would just have to keep a cool finger on the pulse of the community.

Dan sat out the weekend in jail as the judge wouldn't hold a hearing on Saturday to set a bail. The bail hearing on Monday 2 November was before a packed crowd in the small make shift court room. The judge was about to set the bail at $100,000, but the combined lawyers from the Judge Advocate General 's office and the deputy attorney general convinced him that there was sufficient security that Dan was not going to flee. The judge finally gave in and released Dan on his own recognizance.

CHAPTER FIVE
The Big Show in Court

The court hearing to determine if Dan was to be charged with a felony or released with no charges was set for the next Monday 9 November at 10:00 am. Much of the remainder of the day Dan spent with the CIE investigators. He took them to where the shooting had taken place. Several empty casings, 45 caliber casings like the ammunition Dan's side arm fired, were found in the area and among the trees where Dan had been hiding. A few empty rifle shell casings were found on the ground a short distance away. Some rifle slugs were found in the trees where Dan had waited for the possible stalkers. Many fewer casings were found than the probable shots fired. A quick search had obviously been made to remove as much evidence against the two young men as possible.

The two young men were brought in for questioning. Will Parker and Paul Armstrong were considered hostile witnesses and were treated as such. They asked for a lawyer. A public defender had been brought from Denver. They wouldn't talk and refused to submit to a medical examination. So, a phone call to Denver obtained the go ahead to seek the court order for the medical examination. The federal judge read the documents supporting that request. He discussed it briefly with the legal counsel present and issued the order. The order was sent by telegraph to Cleaveland. The doctor waiting for the orders went to the holding areas of the two suspects.

The doctor went first to see Paul Armstrong. It was no surprise that Paul refused to cooperate. The doctor then brought out the medical equipment and two burly uniformed and armed officers came in. They were prepared to hold him while the doctor put him out with an injection. With no other option he finally yielded and began to undress. No injuries were located. They then proceeded to the room where Will Parker was being held and offered him the options available to him. He disrobed without protest. A probable bullet wound was found on his upper right arm. One that had not received proper medical attention.

The judge now in Cleaveland, after seeing the information

presented and issued a warrant allowing a search of the homes and property of both young men. Based on the spent cartridges found at the site of the shooting, the investigators knew what type of rifles they were looking for. The searches took some time but both suspected rifles were found. The rifles, the recovered bullets and spent cartridges were immediately sent to the laboratory in Denver for ballistic tests. They would know the results of those tests tomorrow. Tuesday, the reports on the ballistics tests were received about 3:45 in the afternoon. The rifles had fired the bullets found in the trees around the spot where Dan had been waiting for his probable stalkers.

Will Parker and Paul Armstrong were arrested on suspicion of murder and attempted murder. Their arraignment would take place on Tuesday of next week.

Dan remained free on his own recognizance. The Lieutenant Governor, the National Guard General and his men along with the deputy attorney general went back to Denver. The deputy attorney general would come back next Monday for Dan's court date. The lawyers from the Judge Advocate General's office stayed. Half of the CIE crew were sent back to their respective posts. The military presence in Cleaveland was less intimidating, but still visible. Most of the reporters left as well, many with a promise to return next Monday. Dan was able to spend some nearly peaceful time with his bride.

Sunday, 8 November, when they left for church in Alder Grove, they were accompanied by two deputies from the sheriff's office, to make sure Dan, in his dress uniform, didn't attempt to leave, four members of the CIE and both lawyers from the Judge Advocate General's office. This certainly boosted the numbers in church. Most of the local members were somewhat interested and some were disturbed by their armed presence.

Monday, 9 November, 1953, a large portion of all of the curious and interested observers of last week were again present for the hearing for Dan. Even though no release of information about the case had taken place, the public feeling seemed to be in favor of Dan. The judge was not ignorant of that apparent fact. The court room was packed, with standing room only. The court was called to order and the county judge took his seat. The charges were read, including shooting and injuring a man and carrying a concealed weapon without a license. The judge asked Dan how did he plead, guilty or not guilty.

Dan said, "Not Guilty".

The judge was about to set a date in the future to hear evidence, but one of the federal attorneys requested an immediate hearing as they were prepared to refute those charges and present evidence to support that action. The lawyer stated further that it would not take long for the court to hear and see that evidence. Also, the importance of this case was requiring an inordinate expenditure of time and money of the Department of Defense funds to protect national security in this situation.

The judge was taken by surprise with this turn of events and ordered a ten-minute recess in order to consider this request. After the recess, the judge announced his decision, "I will allow the defense council to proceed with their case. When they are finished if the prosecuting attorney has any evidence to present, he will be allowed to do so."

The lead attorney for Dan, the female Lieutenant Colonel, began by addressing the charge of carrying a concealed weapon without a license. She then presented the legal documents that showed that Dan was a federal law enforcement officer and not only had the right, but was obligated to carry a weapon for self-defense, at all times. This was especially required since at least four attempts to take Dan's life had taken place thus far in Cleaveland.

Dan was allowed or requested to relate to the court about the four incidents, two of which there was no support other than Dan's word for the reported attempts on his life, one the initial attempt to shoot him on Friday October 23 and the attempt to run him down on Monday the 26th.

The other two attempts are well documented and witnesses can be presented if necessary. The first of the two documented attempts of murder was the use of a homemade bomb that had been placed under the pillow on Dan's bed on Friday October 23. A transcript of the phone call in which bomb experts instructed Dan as to how he was to defuse the bomb was presented. The defused and inactivated bomb was presented in evidence. A list of witnesses could testify pertaining to the bomb threat such as: Helmut Schmidt, manager of the ski lodge where the bomb attempt had been made, with the necessity of evacuating the building. And last, the deputy sheriff that carried away the defused bomb.

The second documented attempt on Dan's life is the shootout, again on Friday 23 October. The evidence includes the spent casings found at the incident site, bullets removed from the trees in the area where Dan had waited for his stalkers, and the ballistics reports showing the rifles, found in the homes of the two men in custody on suspicion of murder, had fired the bullets found in the trees in the area where Dan was waiting.

Then Dan was called to the witness stand to tell of his confrontation with the stalkers and his efforts to defend himself without any attempt to kill his stalkers. In other words, he acted in self-defense. He had tried to disarm the two-armed men without any violence nor to attack them. One man armed with a pistol against two men armed with high powered, semiautomatic rifles is not a plausible situation, where Dan would have tried to attack the two-armed men.

Thus, the evidence against the two charges under which Dan had been arrested and held in jail had been presented and they waited for the judge's verdict. The judge immediately dropped the charge of carrying a concealed weapon without a license. But he could not or would not rule on the self-defense plea without further study. A second hearing was set for one week later on Monday the 16th of November 1953 at 10:00 am would convene to consider the final charge. Dan was found not guilty due to self-defense. "Courts Adjourned."

So free, but a limited freedom. Well at least Dan and Grace could be together and not worry about those two killers. But Dan didn't feel that he was as free of them as he would have liked. His warning system, the itch behind his ear was again active. Should he warn Grace or let her relax in peace. The latter for a short time anyway.

As long as he could be sure they were not under attack. When attack possibilities arrived, he would warn her.

Tuesday and Wednesday Dan and Grace laid low and tried to relax, lounging around the lodge with at least two CIE men nearby, trying to be unobtrusive. But evident they were. On Thursday they went to visit Grace's family and let them know that they were okay. The family was a bit curious about the two CIE body guards that were always present. Always present but not always the same men.

Grace's family was interested in Dan and why so much support from the army, and high up support at that. Even the Lieutenant Governor and the General over the states National Guard. "Boy, Dan you must have some pull."

Dan explained as much as he could about himself and his job, which wasn't that much with Dan's top secret security clearance and the nature of his work. What he had to tell them satisfied them for now at least. The young boys seemed adequately impressed. Grace's father asked, "Why does the Colonel, Colonel Oakley, like you so much?"

"When I was first transferred to the Virginia Area Command CIE element, there was the colonel. He wasn't the head of it but was a local administrator for the area command. Some of the enlisted men of an infantry battalion had taken a disliking to him for busting them with stolen property in their possession. They weren't punished as severely as they probably should have been. After their jail term was over they waited for him to leave the headquarters. He was walking away from the area command headquarters when they attacked him. There were six enlisted men against one battle weary colonel. I came upon the attack and waded in, fists flying. I cleared them out rather quickly. Four of them wound up in a hospital before they were tried, given a dishonorable discharge and three-to-five-year prison sentences. The colonel survived and got better fast. He learned when to duck and when to hit hard. He has liked me ever since.

Grace's father and mother, while impressed, were obviously worried and concerned. What had Grace gotten herself into? Dan assured them this would blow over. Then with all of the publicity about him, his work for the CIE element was probably at an end. His position was compromised and this greatly reduced his value to the agency. Dan was nearly up for reenlistment and promotion or being discharged. Under the circumstances the latter is probable. Unless an ROTC position could be found so he wouldn't have to resign his commission.

He would begin a search for a teaching position at some college, hopefully within the area. Then Grace could have opportunity for contact with her family and live a more peaceful life with less stress and fear. Grace seemed to glow at the mention of this prospect. This possibility was even better than to have Dan go into veterinary practice which wasn't the most peaceful life.

On Thursday, Dan received a call from his commander. He wanted Dan back at his post since his involvement in this case was nearly at an end. That would undoubtedly happen on Monday. Dan would probably have to come back and testify and that could be arranged.

Friday Dan and Grace were driving from the lodge to go and visit Graces family again. They lived a few miles out of town. They were just leaving town, with their ever-present rear guards following, when a SUV came out of a side road and rammed them in the side. The SUV had backed up to try and hit them again or escape when the rear guard opened fire on the vehicle. The SUV was stopped and the men in it tried to run on foot. Additional warning fire brought them to a halt. These were not the two suspects. This would require additional investigation.

The deputy sheriff was shortly on the scene. He didn't appear to be the least bit happy with this situation. He had hoped the turmoil over the existing murder case was nearly at an end so his life could be relatively quiet again. He didn't think this was now a likely possibility in the near future. This new case, which probably came under his jurisdiction, would allow him to show that he could handle such cases satisfactorily and that he could protect his part of the county's people. This would be his case if the federal people did not take over. They did not try very hard to take over because they wanted out of this area and leave it to local people.

The deputy took the two men into custody and transported them to the county jail and booked them in on charges of attempted murder. He wondered if these two were involved with the murder of the girl whose body had been found in the canal? And if so, how many others were mixed up in the whole extended mess? Was there a gang of which Paul Armstrong and Will Parker were members? In both circumstances it looked like this whole situation could escalate as long as Dan was in the area.

Dan and Grace were transported to the hospital in Alder Grove where they were checked over to make sure there were no injuries that were more severe but not apparent. They passed with only relatively minor bruises. Grace's car was another matter. It appeared to have been totaled. The frame had been bent and the drive shaft had been broken. The body would almost have to be completely replaced. It would be less costly to buy a new car. This is exactly what they did while they were in Alder Grove. Dan was wondering if his commander would send out an armored car for his use or a Sherman tank. Dan was sure his bodyguard would be doubled. It turned out that Dan was right. Before the day was over the CIE contingency in Cleaveland was at least doubled.

Their visit with Grace's family took place on Saturday rather than on Friday. The family wanted to hear details about this latest attempt on their lives. Grace's parents were not pleased with this continued danger that their new son-in-law and their daughter were subjected to. Dan told them he was being recalled to Quantico. Since he lived on base, neither he nor Grace could even be approached. They would be completely safe.

Also he had been informed that the FBI had been called in on this latest incident. The FBI would likely track down all that might be involved with the attacks on Dan and Grace. With luck the attacks would end while they were at Quantico. Their attendance at church on Sunday also included several armed and uniformed personnel. The local members were not sure they liked this. At least there were visitors that would not likely have any other exposure to this church otherwise.

Monday came as could definitely be expected, and along with the normal advance of days. The next episode of court proceedings was upon them again. The judge had been informed of the latest attempt on the life of Dan and in this latest attempt it included Dan's wife. She was a local and rather popular person. The sentiment was high and in favor of Dan, even if it was only because of his wife. The judge didn't dare issue a guilty verdict against Dan.

His pronouncement of the verdict, "Not Guilty" was met with cheers. The judge had a time to regain quiet in the court room. The court was adjourned.

Arrangements were made for Dan and Grace to leave on Wednesday to return to Quantico, VA. Dan's body guard would be in place up to the plane's departure.

So, Grace still had one day to visit her family. Part of the day was spent in the library to search for colleges and universities in that part of Colorado, and if Dan could get a teaching job there, they would be near Grace's family. And Dan would like that for himself as well as for his wonderful wife. She deserved it.

CHAPTER SIX
CIE Headquarters

Dan reported to the CIE commander on Thursday morning, 19 November 1953. The Colonel told Dan that he and Grace were confined to the post. He didn't want either of them leaving Post where they could be vulnerable to attack or capture. The kidnapping of Grace would be a disaster. They could not let this happen. Dan was temporarily released from duty. A routine procedure. Dan would be free to show Grace around the post.

There would be a hearing into Dan's incident where he shot a man. This also was routine and not expected to have detrimental effects on neither Dan's nor Grace's life. Dan hoped that would indeed be the case. Grace had an eventful first few days of marriage. Dan didn't want that to continue. The hearing was set for Wednesday 25 November at 1330 hours (1:30 pm civilian time).

There was a chapel on the post with The Church of Jesus Christ of Latter-Day Saints services so Dan and Grace will be able to attend. That was some comfort to Grace. And a comfort to Dan as well.

Friday Dan and Grace left the housing area and were walking toward the area where the post businesses were. They were enjoying the balmy fall day. The trees were an array of brilliant reds, oranges and yellows. The air was clear and a slight breeze blowing. Even more they were enjoying each other's company.

That came to an explosive end when a car raced by and shots were fired. Dan was hit and fell to the ground. Grace screamed and dropped to Dan's side. She was frantic and screamed for help. It seemed to be a real long time before she heard sirens in the distance. She also heard running feet coming nearer. She was, by this time, holding Dan's head in her lap. He was unconscious and breathing hoarsely.

Hands lifted her up, against her wishes. She wanted to hold Dan. Police cars and an ambulance arrived and Dan was swiftly examined and loaded into the ambulance. Grace was helped in as well to go with Dan. Dan was moved into the emergency room of the hospital on the post for a determination of his wounds. He had been shot three times. His injuries were serious, more serious than this hospital was equipped to handle. They were going to transfer him by helicopter to the Walter Reed Army Hospital which was one of the best in the US. Dan was stabilized as best possible and as quickly. Then he was wheeled out to the heliport. And he was gone.

Grace was in a state of deep despair and thought of what she had been told, "They would be completely safe at Quantico". Famous last words.

Grace was sitting there in shock when hands touched her again. It was Colonel Oakley. The Colonel told her he would take her to the hospital so she could be near Dan. On the way to the hospital, he informed her that the post had been totally shut down. The shooters would be found. That was little comfort to Grace. Would that save Dan?

The investigation by the CIE and the FBI had taken a dramatic increase in intensity and scope of action. This was more than a simple murder in a small town in Colorado. How wide this problem was is the mystery and question on their minds now. What is behind all of this? Guards will be at Dan's side around the clock and there will be two almost at Grace's side as well. This is not how Grace had envisioned a honeymoon.

Grace called her father and told him what had happened. She asked if he could have a man with the priesthood come and bless Dan? He told her that he would see what could be done. He would make some phone calls and ask for someone to do as Grace wanted.

A number of hours later the head surgeon came out to tell Grace that the surgery to repair Dan's injuries was successful and he should be alright. He would need some time before he is totally recovered but he should be able to have a normal life after that.

Grace leaned over into her lap and cried as she had never done before. She seemed totally helpless and alone. She wanted to see and be with Dan. She was taken into the recovery room so she could be at his side. She was shocked to see him all trussed up, bandaged up and with more tubes coming out of or into his body than she could imagine. "Oh Dan". There wasn't even any space where she could touch him without being covered with bandages, tubes or wires.

A short time later, two men came into Dan's room and introduced themselves. One was Ezra Taft Benson, Secretary of Agriculture and one of the apostles in our Church. The second man was the stake president in the Washington DC. area. They gave a priesthood blessing to Dan. Elder Benson told Grace that Dan would live for the Lord had some important things for Dan to accomplish. He also told Grace, "Your husband is a most remarkable man."

Grace sat by his bed side for hours. Night came on and she continued to keep her vigil on her husband of less than one month. The hospital staff were aware of the situation and were giving her all of the latitude, they could. She dozed off from time to time during the night and woke up in the wee hours of the morning. It is just beginning to get light outside. She awoke and was trying to remember where she was, what the problem was. She heard a whisper, "Grace my love." Dan is awake. She pulled the cord for help. A doctor and some nurses appeared almost immediately.

They begin to check Dan over to make sure he is alright. Things are fine, at least as good or even better than expected. Dan was probably going to be fine. Grace cried again in relief. She wished she could kiss him and hold him, but in his current circumstances, this was not possible.

Finally, when all of the fuss was over Dan told Grace, "*Mafia*." Grace stepped out of the room and found an armed officer posted at the door. She told him, "I must see the Colonel quickly."

"Yes Ma'am", he said and picked up a two-way radio. He spoke to someone and then told her, "He is on his way ".

When the Colonel arrived, he was relieved to learn that Dan was awake. Grace told him, "About the first thing Dan said after he woke up was *Mafia"*

The Colonel was shocked. "How could this be?" The Colonel passed this information to the FBI.

An agent showed up at the hospital about an hour later. By this time Dan was awake enough to talk for short periods of time. The agent, with the Colonel and Grace present, asked Dan, "What makes you think that the Mafia is involved? "

Dan replied, "It is the only thing that makes sense of this whole mess. Check on Bradley Armstrong, the mayor of Cleaveland and a wealthy man. Where did or does he get his money? The job as mayor doesn't pay that well. Also check on Josh Parker, the chief of police in Cleaveland. The two suspects in Cleaveland are the sons of these two men. A simple murder wouldn't cause this much furor. The attacks on me have been half way across this country from one another. This indicates a big organization. The wealth of the mayor implies such a possible connection ".

The agent looked less than confident but he couldn't ignore this information. The bureau would have to get to work on this right away. The three of them left the room and the agent told the Colonel, "If his mind keeps working like this while in his condition, we could use more like him. I only hope this information hits pay dirt ".

The Colonel told the agent, "It is my experience that there is a 90 percent or better chance that it will. Dan has solved more cases for us, the area CIE element, than all others and more by himself than several of the others have together. He was given his position in the CIE element where he could provide the best service to the rest of the group and nation. Dan has this ability, even if I haven't seen it in him under such circumstances, but I would bet my farm that this information is 24 caret gold ".

The last thing the agent said as he was leaving, "I hope you are right."

After we were left alone the Colonel said, "Dan is a national treasure." Then he was gone.

Grace went back in to be with Dan. He was asleep again.

She let him sleep. A nurse came in and asked Grace if she had anything to eat. She told the nurse, "No, but. could I have something?"

The nurse left and shortly came back with a breakfast tray. The food tasted good.

Over the next week Dan gradually got stronger and looked better. The Colonel came to visit with Dan. In the course of time, the Colonel told Dan and Grace, "Your names were being changed. You will be given a plausible story to live by after you leave the hospital. Grace, you will find that Dan's face will look strange to you. He and you have been given new identities. And Dan has been given a new face. All of this to protect the two of you. I'm sorry this had to be done and I hope you will find it okay and forgive me." Grace didn't know what to say. She could only wait and learn who she was. Who they both were.

It turned out that she would be given a new identity also, but It wouldn't require surgery. A different type of cosmetic, hair style, and a change of clothing style and she wouldn't recognize herself. This would be sufficient since her face was not on the front page of all of the newspapers across the nation. A picture would be released to the papers that would steer anyone off her path.

It looked like she and Dan will not be able to attend church in the chapel on the post after all. With this change of identity, how was it going to affect their membership in the Church? How would she be able to have any relationship with her family? All in all, this is such a great turmoil she wondered how she could stand it. But to be without Dan was even worse. She would just have to hold up her chin and do what she could to support Dan. He was going to need all she could give him. This gave her the strength to carry on. Their love for one another would give each of them the strength they would need.

Ten days after Dan's surgery, they removed the bandages. When Grace saw Dan, she almost gasped, but she had been training herself to do no such thing. Dan was different. Different enough that I could have gasped, but he was still good looking. I didn't want to show any reaction that might imply that I didn't love him. I did love him, but I would have to have a little time to get used to him again.

He was still Dan and I had to get used to him just like I had to get used to him at first. I did get used to him even though I was a bit scared of him then. I can do it again and my love for him, Dan or whomever he is and whomever I am, will grow even stronger. This is also strange to me that I am now a different person, yet I'm not. I'm still Grace Jorgensen. That is still almost as strange as well. There have just been too many changes in a short time to adjust to them in such a fast pace. I just have to remember who I married.

Dan was stronger now and could get up and walk around. Grace would walk with him and put her arm around him. He seemed to like that. He didn't take to the change of his face well and was often sullen. We haven't gotten used to our new names yet either. Richard and Doris Stierwalt. That is going to take some getting used to. Maybe they could change that to Stewart. I'll talk to Richard and see what he thinks of that. There is still time for us to make up our minds before our names become permanent.

It has been five days since Richard has been up and around. We talk and once in a while he even smiles like he always used to. We have decided on the name of Stewart. The Colonel approved so we are now Richard and Doris Stewart. We are getting accustomed to that even if not totally accepting it. But if this can help us live a "safe" life, then let it be. At least I hope it works out that way...

It has been a month now and Richard is almost back to normal, at least a modified normal. We are expecting the Colonel to show up and visit us today.

Being in this hospital or whatever it is, is almost like being in prison. We don't really know where we are. They had loaded us into a van, with no windows and the windshield blocked from our view. We were driven around for a while and then they took us into the underground garage of this building. We have windows to see out of but all we can see is trees and more trees.

The Colonel visited us today. He told us, "Will Parker and Paul Armstrong were broken out of jail. There was a vehicle waiting for them and they took off, driving faster than they ought to. They came to a sharp turn in the road by a rather long drop into a ravine. They evidently stepped on the brake, but no brakes. They went over the edge and were both killed. It looks like a set up to get rid of them before they talked. This whole thing is one mess. We need your brain to figure this out ".

"The FBI has looked into the finances of Bradley Armstrong and things are definitely crooked. They may have enough on him soon to indict him. Josh Parker also seems to be sweating a bit. We'll have both of them but how far can we go up the chain?"

Dan, or Richard now, thought of Victor Hugo again. In *Les Miserables,* Victor Hugo stated, *"The guilty one is the one who caused the sin."* Who has caused this sin? If Richard can have his say, the one who caused all of this sin will pay. Doris could feel his feelings and interpret them. She thought, "Richard is getting bitter. What can I do to stop this bitterness? This bitterness can cause more sin and that would make Richard guilty."

After spending another month in their second "prison", they were told where they were going. There was a college in Colorado where they needed a biology teacher and a part time ROTC instructor. Richard will be Lieutenant Colonel Richard Stewart. Richard Stewart, Professor!? That is funny.

"The enrollment is not large and the school will be happy to have Richard, especially since the Army will be paying your salary. There is a nice home there for you and it is a nice quiet place in a beautiful setting. There will be a few individuals on campus to watch after you for a while. Just to make sure our witness protection scheme works. We will make sure your personal items will be shipped to you so that you can alter them as you wish to make sure your true identity is safe ".

"Your cover story as you know is that you were injured in a battle in Korea with multiple gunshot wounds. You are now back in the harness. We hope the peaceful atmosphere of this college will be good for you and help you to get back to being yourself. The name doesn't change who you are ". They left two day later for their new abode. Richard had to use a cane to walk but he was getting stronger and actually getting some of his humor back. He was also starting to pay more attention to Doris. The love returning to his eyes.

Doris could feel it and his bitterness was waning away slowly. She only hoped it would disappear, the sooner the better.

They arrived in their new home which was back against a mixed maple and spruce forest. There were plenty of trails they could explore where it was peaceful and quiet. You could hear the birds singing and from time to time the chatter and scolding of squirrels. Their home had two stories. For a while this would cause Richard some problems but we had a bedroom on the main floor. After about a week in our new home, Richard woke up one morning, looked at Doris and leaned over and kissed her heartily. This was new for Richard and Doris was elated. That day it was almost like Dan was alive again. Even if Dan were now Richard. Richard was much like Dan had been. They went for long walks and talked about themselves and what they could do. Richard was getting back some of his enthusiasm and drive. This place was just what we needed.

School started September 7 and Richard entered into his new task like he was meant to be a teacher. What he enjoyed most about this job was the ability to spark the curiosity and the interest of the students to think and learn. True intelligence is being able to think and discover new ideas within yourself. To come up with new ideas rather than to just regurgitate what someone else thought of. To be able to take two unrelated subjects or fields of study and put them together to fit into something completely different. That is intelligence, not just memory. This requires a person to learn to think for himself or herself.

Richard was coming to life. Then one day, 7 December, Richard was reading a newspaper and came across an article. The headline of the article read, **Body of young woman found with two right shoes.** The article went on to say that she had not been identified. Means of death unknown but she had been dead for months which made it difficult to come to any conclusions other than foul play was strongly suspected. This article sparked another fire in Richard. He was going to try to help find the guilty one at the top. *"The guilty one is the one who caused the sin"*.

If he did not try to help, then he Richard, was part of those that caused the sin. To be able to do something and just sit back and do nothing was being part of the cause of the sin. He was not going to be the cause of this sin. He got up and called the Colonel at CIE. The Colonel told Richard, "You are foolish to call me and draw attention to yourself again ". Richard agreed that he couldn't do much of anything in the field or even in the CIE office, but "I can still think. I can analyze information and help put the pieces of this puzzle together. *"The guilty one is the one who caused the sin".* And he said, *"I, Richard, am not going to be part of the cause of this sin."*

Richard was alive again, and controlled his anger and drive to solve this heinous sin. He noticed Doris more often and his show of affection was more like he used to be. This helped Doris even more to help Richard. She could enter into his drive to help solve this crime. One that had turned her life totally upside down. Another thing that helped Doris is they now had a way to communicate with her family. The devastation of Doris's life had a terrible impact on her parents and family. The damage of one sinful act can hurt many people. The ripples of damage spread outward like the ripples on a pond when a pebble is tossed into the water. In this case it wasn't a pebble, it was a boulder. In actuality it was more than a boulder, it was a series of boulders.

Richard's drive didn't stop him going for walks with Doris, hand in hand. He kissed her frequently and just held her tight. When Richard held Doris in his arms it felt almost like a charge of electricity flowing though him, recharging him. Richard's love for Doris grew and grew. Doris meant the world to him. Doris was his world. Richard and Doris were in this to the end, together. Poor pity the guilty, Dan was onto their scent like a blood hound, "Excuse my language!? But, Bring the SOBs down"

CHAPTER SEVEN
Come What May

A few days after calling the Colonel, now 16 December, a man came to their door. He was dressed in a pair of coveralls. He informed them quietly, that he was from the FBI and had some questions for them. He was dressed as he is so no one would connect him with the FBI and put them at risk. They asked for his ID and then let him in. Richard picked up the phone and called the Colonel and asked him about this man. The man was the real thing. The FBI agent then kind of chastised Richard for letting him in so easily. That was when Richard showed him his Colt 45, cocked and loaded. Had the agent made one false move he would have been one second or less from being a sieve.

"So, let's get down to business." the agent said. I understand that you are willing to help us. Your Colonel tells us you have a remarkable ability to see things, analyze complex information and make heads and tails of it and figure out what it all means. I can tell you this whole case is a can of worms. You suggested that we look into the financial situation of Bradley Armstrong. Why?"

Richard told the FBI Agent, "He is the mayor of Cleaveland, which doesn't provide any great income. Yet he seems to have money to burn. His son had everything he wanted and the best, but the son apparently had no independent source of income. This causes a flag to start waving. What is the source of his income? His son was one of the ones that tried to kill me. The conclusion that I came to about that is that the father didn't try to discipline the son. Is the son just doing what the father does? After I was shot and I began to come around the idea was in my mind. The Mafia. I think there is a connection. That could even tie in with the attempt to kill me at Quantico. That would require an organization. Maybe not the Mafia but something close to it."

The agent whistled. "Wow, you've done more in your head than a whole passel of agents in the field. By the way we have been able to tie Bradley Armstrong with a drug cartel that is an off shoot of the Mafia. I think we are closing in on one of the ring leaders. We will soon know."

"So now" said Richard, "How about the police chief, Josh Parker, what have you found out about him?"

"We haven't been able to find anything that we could prosecute him for. Do you have anything on him?"

"No, just that he hasn't kept much of a leash on his son and that is too late now, since he is dead. His death I could attribute to the Mafia or whatever gang he was tied into. I think the main problem there is or was the chief's wife. I'm sure Will was the apple of her eye and he wanted to out shine his best friend, Paul Armstrong."

"So, you think that the deaths of Paul Armstrong and Will Parker were done by the off shoot of the Mafia?"

Richard replied, "Just look at the circumstances. They are in jail and have been tied up tight as a drum in the attempted murder of me. The nearly fatal attack on me takes place 2000 miles away from Cleaveland within two days after I left and supposedly ensconced at Quantico. That arrangement takes organization, a big organization. Then the two boys are broken out of jail and provided with a getaway vehicle. In their frantic drive to freedom, they go around a sharp bend with a deep drop off on the outside of the bend. The driver steps on the brake to slow down for the turn and, walla, there are no brakes. Is that a coincidence? I don't think so. A pair of potential stool pigeons is eliminated. A pair that had no further value to their establishment. Now agent Reynolds, I think you had something specific to discuss with me. Spill it."

Agent Reynolds looked at Doris and rather shyly said he didn't think it was appropriate for a woman's ears.

Doris spoke up and said, "Do you think you have anything to say that I didn't hear as a police officer for several years?"

"Alright", the agent said, "but it isn't pleasant. We think there is a leak either in the FBI or at CIE. We recommend you take a powder for a while and give us some time to ferret out the stool pigeon ".

"That sounds okay, but I have an idea that might help you. Tell any potential suspected person, like under the table, a false trail that I am going to appear at some news release event at some specific place. Then do the same for each suspect except each suspect is given a different place and a different time. Then watch the various false news release spots for suspicious individuals. The spot where potential assassins show up will then tell you who the traitor is."

"In the mean time I will take a powder. Doris and I will go to a place of my or our selection and just stay out of sight. When the coast is clear, put a news release out to the TV stations that the CIE commander has been put on administrative leave for some made up reason. The Colonel will cooperate."

After the agent left Richard packed a few things, then we got in our car and drove away. We went not much farther than one half mile and Richard pulled into a small lane in the woods, he drove to the end, maybe just over one-half mile. We got out of the car, which Richard locked up, and then followed a path. The path took us right back to our home. It was dark by now so we were able to get to the back door of our home and enter without being seen. We turned no lights on and went to bed.

The next day we stayed in and kept vigil, not letting any sign show we were home. About 10:30, the "FBI agent" came to our home again, dressed in coveralls like a utility repairman. He let himself in the house and started for our bedroom. Dan, or Richard, stepped out from the kitchen about the time the intruder, whom ever he was, reached for the door knob. Dan ordered him to stop. Dan had his 45 in his hand. The intruder, the supposed FBI agent, whirled and tossed the bag he was carrying at Dan. Dan fired and ducked the bag. The intruder fell to the floor. He wasn't going anywhere. He swore at Dan and died. We looked in the bag and found a bomb. Dan left the bag where it fell and called the Colonel.

Two CIE officers were at our home within two hours. They recognized the dead man. He was an FBI agent, or had been until a few days ago when he was fired. Another attempt to get rid of me foiled. We called the police and reported the shooting.

This caused no small ruckus. We knew there would be an investigation and probably an inquest. The CIE officers took the bomb away. It was obvious that our cover was no longer of any benefit. So, what do we do now? My conclusion was to go on as if nothing had happened. But, was that the best? There was the old phrase, *"The best defense was a good offense."* Grace and I talked things over and first of all we wanted our own identities back.

I called the Colonel and talked it over with him, telling him of our decision to have our own identities back. Reluctantly he agreed. Now, where ever we were to go, we would have two tags along. Our body guards. The dangers were not over.

The first move or action we needed was for me to go to the president of the school where I worked and lay things on the line. So, on 20 December I told the school president of my real identity and told him about the attempts on my life and the one that just happened. I also told him of the risks of me staying on at the school. I would be glad to stay if he agreed and I gave him a week to think it over.

Our next move was to go and visit Grace's family. Grace missed them greatly. It was Tuesday 22 December and we drove over there. We had a joyous reunion which turned fearful as it dawned on Grace's parents of the implications of us being Dan and Grace again. But we could communicate freely again, which was a great relief.

We then drove up to the lodge to visit Helmut and Gretta. When we walked in, there was Chief Parker standing there, his revolver in his hand. He said, with anger in his voice and anger plastered all over his face, "You killed my son. Now, it's your turn." But he didn't seem able to pull the trigger and his hand was shaking like a leaf in a wind. I walked up to him and gently removed the pistol from his hand. He then broke down and sobbed. After he was able to recover himself, we talked. He knew what had been going on but his wife wouldn't hear of it. Her son, the apple of her eye and life, he couldn't do what they were saying about him. She was now in a mental hospital totally living in what she believed to be. Living in a total fantasy.

I asked him how he knew that I would be at the lodge at

this time. "Someone told me you were in the area and visiting the Herndon family. I figured that it wouldn't be long before you came to the lodge to see the Schmidts. And I was right. But I couldn't do what I told myself I had to do".

"I didn't kill Will, he killed himself. A person creates most of his own problems by trying to ignore what his own actions produce. When we stick our heads in the sand, figuratively, we hope the problems we are facing will just blow away. But they don't. Will on the other hand was filled with the desire to be bigger and more powerful than his *best friend*, Paul Armstrong. He would follow Paul almost like a puppy dog and let himself be drawn into trouble over his head. We show by our decisions what we really are. And Will just needed the opportunity to be free of Paul to make his own decisions and prove to himself what he really was. Too late now.'

Chief Parker said, "The mayor had been arrested, to the shock of the town. He could not have been doing what he was arrested for. He did so many good things for the town. The FBI investigation of his finances, at your recommendation, showed that a lot of his money came by way of an off-shoot of the Mafia for drug trafficking and money laundering. He's got secure accommodations for some time to come. A new mayor, this will require the dust to settle and the chance for everyone to consider who might make the best mayor and who was willing to take on the task. I am still the chief, still in office, basically on probation".

Despite what had happened, he had been able to pull himself together and was doing an excellent job for the town. The big question for Dan was how many of the Mafia gang were still in the area? Whoever they were, they didn't seem to have long life expectancies.

They were back to the college. With his real name and his history known, he drew a far different stare these days when he walked about town and on campus. It was like a breath of fresh air to think and do, using his real name. Dan went to see the school president again. President Wilson realized the dangers that were involved with keeping Dan on as a teacher. He also was aware of what Dan was doing for the students. He was a remarkable teacher. Dan might scare some away, but he would draw more in than left, and those he attracted would be students that every school would want. He had discussed this whole situation with the board of governors and they agreed. They wanted to keep Dan as a teacher. Their school security would need to be beefed up. Perhaps the Army could help there.

Dan was pleased and gratified by their decision and especially the reason why they decided as they did. *Gird up your loins, the battle looms and I'm in for the battle and the duration.* No one, and I intend to make sure that no one drives me out or defeats me.

Monday 3 January, Dan began wearing his uniform on campus, and with approval, he was armed and loaded. This seemed to intimidate a few students but heightened the interests of his ROTC students. Plus, his classes increased in size. The school would have to find a larger class room for him. The students took little time to accept the uniformed or plain clothed and armed guards that were with Dan all of the time. Dan's ROTC students were starting to wear side arms, loaded. A number of other students were also. The school's firing range was getting a lot more use these days. The campus was becoming to be one loaded for bear, and hoping for a chance at the bear. The big question was, "When will the climax come?"

About three weeks after Dan's true identity came out, Tuesday 25 January, as Dan was walking across campus a drive by shooting was attempted. There were at least two shooters in the car, fortunately Dan was not injured. The shooters were caught in a hail storm of pistol fire. The assassins never survived the day out. Fortunately, due to training of the entire student body and all of the staff had received, when the shooting started every one dropped to the ground or floor. There had been no injuries of students or staff from friendly fire.

If the attention the campus received after I shot and killed the former FBI agent was overwhelming, it was nothing compared to this one. Campus police, city police, County sheriff's officers, state police, FBI and CIE officers converged on the campus and interviewed all that had taken part in the shooting, and many that had not.

Attacking Dan on campus was like sticking your head into a wasp's nest. Painful and life threatening. The school quickly became well known nationwide. And that notoriety extended to foreign shores as well. This would likely attract an interesting student body. That evening Dan and Grace were talking about this whole problem and who might be behind all of these attacks on Dan. An FBI agent appeared at their door, a real FBI agent. The agent and Grace both wanted the same thing and Grace asked, "Was there anyone at CIE that had it in for you. Dan? The person behind all of these attacks seemed to be a fanatic. And a deranged one at that."

Dan said, "The only one I can think of was Lieutenant Colonel Robert Nash, the deputy commander of the CIE. He was always jealous whenever I got an award of some kind or another. He was a good officer and when he became deputy commander, I think he figured he could lord it over me. But the commander didn't put Robert in my chain of command, or me in his chain of command. I answered only to the commander. Bobby (which he was known as behind his back) whenever I received any recognition, his offense toward me blew up, even more than it already was. His hatred of me has caused him to be obsessed with trying to put me down. He doesn't do his job properly as the deputy commander of the CIE. Which is causing his appraisals and ratings to drop. If this continues, he may receive a dishonorable discharge. I think he would do anything to hurt me in any way he could. I can think of no one else. It could be Bobby didn't seem to have the guts or intelligence to plan any such kind of attack that I have experienced ".

The rest of their discussion resulted in no added possibilities and that one which didn't appear to carry enough weight to attract much attention, was the only one left. What do we do? The agent took this new information with him for investigation.

It was near evening and it looked like there would be a fantastic sunset. They both loved sunsets so they went for a walk. It was late enough in the winter that all of the leaves had fallen but the trees seemed to be on fire in the reddish glow of the setting sun. The sky was an array of colors that a person had a difficult time imagining such colors. Dan began to tell Grace of a sunset he had seen as a child. "The sunset was so spectacular that my father called the entire family out to see it. We all sat on the porch of our house and watched the sunset for about fifteen minutes. I can't even begin to describe the colors of that sunset. My dad would sometimes do something like that, I think so his children could at least have some wonderful memories."

Dan continued in his slow walk into the night, contemplating the memories of his life. Grace had her attention on Dan, considering his delving into his past. He didn't talk much about his past and family. His parents had evidently been proud of Dan, at least his mother was, but his brother did not accept Dan for what he was and always put him down. It was now dark so they walked back to their home. A comforting thought, our home. They called it quits and went to bed. All in all, not a bad day.

They did not have trouble sleeping. Their sleep was that of two peaceful hearted people. They slept snuggled up against one another as if they couldn't stand to be apart. The way it should be. The way husbands and wives should always be.

CHAPTER EIGHT
Is This The Bitter End

The next couple of weeks went by with as little excitement and fanfare as one could ever hope for, Dan and Grace were able to spend more time together in peace. It even got to the point where they expected peace and tranquility each day. Dan realized this could get dangerous. Were they being put off guard to make them more vulnerable for another attempt on his life. Or worse, an attempt on the life of Grace. The most abominable thing the low life could do.

Wednesday 6 April, Dan and Grace began spending more time at the firing range. Dan was an expert marksman with pistol or rifle, but he couldn't let himself become complacent. He knew Grace was pretty good with a pistol, but he was startled when he watched her fire. She was fast and accurate. Dan wasn't sure he could beat her in a shooting match. She was calm, steady, fast and placed her shots where she wanted them. If anyone came at her, poor pity them.

Dan's work with the students seems to have become his passion. He was like Socrates. He wanted to teach the truth and teach the students how to think for themselves. How to make good choices in life and become a benefit for humanity rather than a parasite. There were some signs of success among the students for which Dan was pleased.

The time passed in peace for a few more weeks. Then one day, Wednesday 27 April, Grace was opening some mail when she called to Dan, "Dan come look at this." She showed him an envelope with an off-white powder in it. Dan carefully closed the envelope and asked for a large envelope or bag. Grace got one and Dan put the closed envelope into it and folded the top closed carefully also. Then he told Grace to wash her hands thoroughly. He did the same, then called the Colonel and told him about the envelope.

Colonel Oakley immediately placed a call to Fort Detrick Maryland. Fort Detrick was the place where a lot of work was done by the Army during World War II in preparation of possible biological warfare attacks, including anthrax. They would have some help at Dan's home before the day was out. The suspicious envelope was to be left alone and all of the area where it was opened needed to be wiped down with a strong bleach solution, this includes the floor and counter tops. This included their hands and arms. Protective doses of penicillin must be started immediately. The penicillin would be delivered by the Fort Detrick personnel and both of them should start on it immediately. The main concern is anthrax. The penicillin should take care of it.

The Fort Detrick personnel arrived later that day. They donned masks, gloves and disposable coveralls. They took the sack with the envelope inside and set up a small isolation chamber on the table and opened the bag and then the envelope. They put some of the dust on a microscope slide, fixed it, stained it and covered the slide with a glass cover slip. They rinsed the slide in a disinfectant and brought the slide out of the chamber and examined the slide under a microscope. The specimens looked something about like anthrax alright. It would take time to confirm this analysis. The Fort Detrick crew then began to cleanup and disinfect the area where the envelope had been opened. And where Dan and Grace had been since the envelope had been opened. This whole process took all of the remaining daylight and into the night.

When the crew left, they gave Dan enough penicillin to dose himself and Grace for ten days. In addition, they said they would have a lab report on the dust in about four days. They would then know for sure what this stuff was. We were asked to not leave the house. After the Fort Detrick group left Dan began to catalog the attempts on his or their lives:

    1 - Rifle fire   Dan
    2 - Rifle fire   Dan
    3 - Bomb   Dan
    4 - Attempted run over by pickup   Dan
    5 - Rammed by SUV   Dan & Grace
    6 - Shot 3 times   Dan
    7 - Bomb   Dan & Grace
    8 - Shooting   Dan
    9 - Anthrax?   Dan & Grace

Dan and Grace then proceeded to wash any clothing they were wearing at the time the powder was discovered, any rugs in the area, and any linens in the area where the powder was discovered. All of which was to reduce the chance of anthrax being in the home.

Thinking the coast was clear Grace looked out the front window, gasped and called out to me, "Dan come and look at this ". On looking out the window I saw a couple of signs stuck up in the lawn, Quarantined, Anthrax Suspect. This was great. Now we would really be shunned.

A call a couple of days later brought good news, the powder was not anthrax spores. It turned out to be a type of flour. Dan then called the school president and informed him that it turned out to be a hoax. He was relieved. He called the Colonel and who informed him that Fort Detrick had told him first. How many false alarms are there going to be, and how many real attacks will there to be? This is getting to be ridiculous.

Later that day Dan taught a fantastic lesson in biology. The question had been brought up by a student, "Why can wading birds stand in salt water that was below freezing and not lose its feet from frost bite?"

Dan explained, "First of all, the blood of such birds probably had sufficient salts in the blood that it and the cells of the feet did not freeze. Second, the birds did not suffer because their core body temperature did not drop. Loss of core body heat is the primary cause of death. The bird's body temperature is maintained with the feet in freezing water by a system known as counter current exchange. The warm blood being pumped down the legs travels down through arteries. Immediately adjacent to the artery is a vein carrying blood back to the body and to the heart. The blood in the artery is warm and the blood in the vein is cold. As the venous blood flows up alongside of the arterial blood, the heat of the arterial blood is transferred to the venous blood. The arterial blood is cooled as it goes down and the venous blood is warmed as it is pushed up to the body. So, the body doesn't lose much heat. "

ROTC was definitely another type of class. There were from five to eight students in each of the four years of school for a total of 28 ROTC students. They were supposed to learn the basic history of the Army and how to disassemble an M1 Garand military rifle and be able to put it together again. They were to be able to do the same with a 30-caliber light machine gun and also a 50-caliber machine gun. The latter gun being more difficult and dangerous. They were to fire 22 caliber rifles on the rifle range and learn close order drill. All of that was old stuff and they liked it, but then they would ask questions about the Criminal Investigation Element (CIE) and I would tell them what I could. This was their primary interest. It was as if I were training the next generation of CIE officers.

Another class Dan was asked to teach was that of self-defense. There were twenty-five in this class, seventeen males and eight females. This made for an interesting and challenging set up. A person would think the females were at a disadvantage. But his experience with this class taught him that this was not so. The girls did not hold back on punches and were aggressive. Seven out of ten matches between a boy and a girl, the girl would have the boy on the floor in less than fifteen seconds. If the boy was able to put the girl down, it took about twenty-five seconds. Dan didn't want to have to face those girls. And those girls were good looking, petite young ladies. They were just not afraid.

Then one day there was a special event and Dan had the ROTC classes and the biology class together. The classes that day were shorter than normal because of the event, so Dan decided that the combined class would be a totally question and answer session. And what questions they came up with. "Have you ever killed a man?"

"Yes, and it is an experience you hope you will never have to go through again."

"How long have you been married?"

"About four and a half years."

"Is this your first marriage?"

"No, my first wife was killed in London in 1945 due to a

buzz bomb explosion."

"What is a buzz bomb?"

"A buzz bomb is a large bomb with wings and a pulse jet attached. The Germans built them, put enough fuel in them to reach a specific target, usually a large city. They would aim them at the city they wanted to hit, start the pulse jet and launch them at their targets. They were called buzz bombs because of the noise the pulse jets produced. When the buzz stopped, you had better have a safe shelter handy. My wife did not."

This went on and on, far longer than I would have liked. But I had to do what I had promised the students. You have to keep your promises, that is if you want the students to have any confidence or trust in you. By enduring the time to answer questions that most people would have considered as impertinent he hoped that it would help to build the confidence and trust among the students in himself. If you can gain the student's confidence, this will often carry the weight with the staff as well.

As Dan was leaving his class room, followed by a mass of students, a man rushed at him, brandishing a rather large knife. Dan turned quickly to face his assailant. The man lunged at Dan swinging the blade in and up trying to disembowel him. Dan turned to the side, allowing the blade to pass within millimeters of his body, and struck down with the heal of his hand. This knocked the knife from the assailant's hand and broke his wrist. The would-be killer fell to the floor, holding his broken wrist and wailed, "You broke my wrist".

Dan replied, "You're lucky I didn't pull my 45, you would be dead if I had".

His students filed from the class room and stood gaping at Dan and the knife man. They decided they would never cross their teacher. And many were impressed how simply and quickly he defended himself. It wasn't long before the campus and city police were on site. They questioned Dan and then carted the so-called tough guy away, first to the hospital and then to jail. When is this ever going to end? When will they leave him alone to teach.

Later, his class of self-defense increased in popularity and attendance. He wanted to teach these young people to think for themselves. He wanted them to have an education with a broad base. Specialists learn more and more about less and less until they know everything about nothing. The system either does that or they ruin the students' ability to think out of the box. The accepted way of teaching the students was be able to repeat what someone else said or did. The students were to accept the rut as they were taught and not try to get out of it. The teaching of mediocrity.

If the teachers teach mediocrity, we wind up as a mediocre nation. This nation didn't start out to be such. The people had to work, sweat tears and blood to be a nation. Hopefully this can be a nation of integrity. Not a pack of thieves. A wise man, Major John Stierwalt of the Air Force, once told me, "The value of education begins with the education of values".

It had been about one week since the anthrax hoax and he and Grace were getting pretty antsy. And now it has been five days after the anthrax scare that the knife attack happened. We wondered, what next? The unknown is harder to face than almost any known danger, they weren't complaining that we were not under constant attack, but being on edge ready for attack can be wearing. Were the attacks over? Was the king pin dead? They were sure he, or she, was not. Time would tell.

Grace and I spent the better part of the next couple of days rehashing the history and trying to place together the pieces of this puzzle. One time we considered Lieutenant Colonel Robert Nash, the deputy commander of CIE, as the king pin behind these attacks on me. I felt that he wasn't up to arranging such a series of attacks.

We also considered Josh Parker, the Chief of Police of Cleaveland. When he confronted me in the foyer of the Cleaveland ski lodge, he couldn't hold his pistol on me, he was so unsteady. He let me take it away from him with no resistance and after he calmed down, he told me pretty much everything with no malice in his voice. His reaction that time didn't seem that he could or would have really arranged attempts on Dan's life.

The next person on our suspect list was the former mayor of Cleaveland, Bradley Armstrong. The beefy man plunged toward Dan a while back with his fists balled up and snorting like a raging bull. He swung his fist at Dan, this in the foyer of the lodge. Another thing he threatened me with was "I'll show you who I am. I own this town and I run it as well. I'm the mayor and I'll have you arrested within the hour." His anger was such that he could have put out a contract on Dan's life. The problem with this is he is in jail. But he could have set up a contract on Dan's life which could continue after he was arrested. The main problem there is that when he was arrested and sentenced, much of his wealth that was in the banks and property was confiscated. So, there wasn't the money to sustain a contract. He may have been involved at first but not for long. His reaction when he faced Dan in the lobby of the lodge and his threat would support the theory of him starting the contract on Dan's life.

Dan and Grace were unable to go any further along that line of thinking about who was the king pin in this plot to kill Dan. Might they also expand their plot to attack Grace to hurt me. He hoped not. In spite of the conclusions, they have arrived at, when you really look at the information, we really had to leave Lieutenant Colonel Robert Nash on the plate. He may not have everything he needs to carry out such a task, but he is capable of obtaining the necessary backing. He would know about the Mafia and their splinter groups and probably some contacts. He is possibly furious enough with Dan to make contact with someone and place a contract on Dan. He could provide critical information to the Mafia to make his payments.

So, all in all, it looks like Lieutenant Colonel Robert Nash has all that is needed to be no.1 on the list. Grace asked Dan, "Why did the Lieutenant Colonel Robert Nash hate you so much?"

Dan told her that this dated back six long years ago, or longer. The Army, in its infinite wisdom had created a position as chief of investigations. Robert Nash figured he already had his foot in the door. He received his promotion as Lieutenant Colonel about ten days before I did. Therefore, he had seniority over me and figured it to be automatic for him to be the chief of investigations. However, the Commander made me the chief of investigations, Robert's job if you take his word for it. Then when he was made deputy commander, he figured he would be able to brow beat me and lord it over me. But the CIE Commander, Colonel Oakley made me chief of investigations and initially left me out of the normal chain of command. I answered only to Colonel Oakley, not to Robert Nash. All of these incidents, are believed to have caused him to have a burning and fierce hatred for me.

If a person allows something like this to get inside of themselves, it grows like cancer. They become so tied into the hatred that they no longer function correctly. Instead of growing and progressing, they develop heart rot like a tree. Then when the winds of adversity come along, they don't have the strength to survive the blast of the winds of adversity. They come down. That seems to be where Robert Nash is now. "He is dangerous and could have sold out to the Mafia to get at me." Dan told Grace, "You need to be careful my love. He could decide to come after you to hurt me. I think he may be that despicable ".

A couple of weeks later, Grace had finished recording some family information on her tape recorder which she put in one of the pockets of her maternity smock and then checked her revolver. A 38 special. One that she liked and was good at handling of this pistol with speed, steadiness and accuracy... She finished with the gun and the doorbell rang. Grace slipped the gun into the most convenient place, the other pocket in her smock. She was not just a little pregnant. She was very pregnant. She was due in about three weeks.

She walked, or should I say, waddled, to the front door. Grace opened the door and saw a uniformed army officer. He was a Lieutenant Colonel, like Dan. He asked if Dan were at home, I told him no. I also told him, "I have to leave in about five minutes so I cannot invite you in at the time ". She asked him, "Could you come back at 5:30 when Dan would be home, I'm sure Dan would love to see you ". He didn't answer. She started to push the door closed but he shoved the door open and pushed Grace back. Then he stepped into the room. He looked around with an evil look on his face and a wicked smile.

"Well Dan has a cozy little place here and an even more cozy wife to come home to. Isn't that nice. I'll bet you two have fun in bed. You look like he has humped you plenty. When I get through with you, you won't be so pretty and attractive to Dan. And then I will finish Dan off ".

This was Lieutenant Colonel Robert Nash, the deputy commander of CIE. Grace had turned on the tape recorder when he pushed into the room and she hoped that enough of what he was saying was being picked up. He continued his vulgar promises of what he was going to do to Grace and then to Dan. He was bragging and enjoying all of it. He was doing all he could think of to scare her. It did some, but even more it made her mad. Mad that any man could dream of such evil and terrible things to do to another human being. He was a total bundle of hatred.

He continued to push Grace back but paid no attention as to where she was going. He pulled his side arm and waved it around. He said, "See this little toy I have. A Colt 45. You can't escape it nor can you escape me. When I am through with you, you will wish you were dead. "Grace just kept backing to get to the location of the telephone. This took a bit of time. She didn't retreat rapidly, but retreated methodically to try to reduce as much of his advantage over her as possible.

He kept bragging that Dan was a flash in the pan, but he would come down. "And I, Robert Nash, will bring him down. I have had all kinds of thugs going after him. They all failed. I had an ex-FBI agent try to blow the both of you up, but he couldn't do it. I've had gun experts try to kill him only to goof it. I had one of the best with a knife go for Dan and he couldn't carry it off either. But I will kill him myself. And then we'll see who is the big shot at the CIE ".

Periodically, Bobby, as Dan called him, would make a sudden dash to catch me. I was able to slip out of his reach and got some advantage over him in doing so. This infuriated him. As Grace continued to back away from him, she looked at the clock, 4:45. Dan should be home soon.

She heard what was probably a neighbor's car door slam. Colonel Nash quickly turned away for a second. During that time Grace had her revolver in her hand and it was pointed at the creep's heart, if he had one. This startled him and he paused for a moment. During this pause Grace lifted the phone at her elbow and when the operator came on, she asked for the police. The desk sergeant answered the phone and Grace identified herself and gave her address. She then told the Sergeant, "Hurry, I have just shot an intruder" and hung up. The Lieutenant Colonel had a shocked look on his face, he lifted his gun, and Grace fired.

The police arrived within three minutes. They came swarming into the house. Took one look at the Lieutenant Colonel on the floor and turned-on Grace with a surprised look on their faces. She was slumped down in a chair. The way she felt, she was sure that she had quit an ashen complexion. She handed them her pistol and then her tape recorder. Then she said, "I hope this is all on the tape. I don't feel much like answering questions just now ".

A moment or so later, Dan came busting in through the front door. He took one look at "Bobby" lying on the floor, then he looked at Grace and went over and knelt down beside the chair she had fallen into. Dan then told the police Lieutenant, "If you don't mind Lieutenant, we will come down to the station in the morning and give complete statements. This after my wife has had a chance to recover. I don't think she ever shot a person before while working as a police officer. I think she needs some time to recover and then she will be able to talk with you ".

The lieutenant said, "I think that will be alright. We have the pistol she used and a tape recorder that we hope will have a complete recording of what went on. If the recording is good, then we probably won't need much from her tomorrow. We will need what information you can give us about this guy from you as well. Who is he?"

Dan told him, "He is Lieutenant Colonel Robert Nash, deputy commander, CIE. He has hated me for years. I think he finally flipped his lid. I think it best if you call CIE headquarters and inform Colonel Oakley. He can tell you more about him than I can, I'm sure. In fact, if you asked him, I'll bet he would come here quickly."

That night didn't bring peace. At least not right away. Dan and Grace talked well into the night and they both unburdened ourselves of baggage that they didn't need to be packing around.

They talked, then Dan held Grace in his arms until she fell asleep... They woke up a bit later in the morning than usual, but they woke up freer of baggage than ever before and deeper in love. They were one.

They went to the police station, the Police Chief and the Lieutenant were there to greet us. Dan wondered if they were in trouble and displayed a bit of anxiety. The chief broke into the broadest and brightest smile Dan had ever seen. He thanked us for coming in and he wanted us to know of his gratitude for our service to their town and school. President Wilson came in and he brought a delegation of students from the College, including the entire ROTC group as well as many of Dan's other students. The mayor presented Grace with a medal of honor of the students' making, for her heroism in the face of an armed enemy. That is exactly what she was. The students then gave Dan a round of cheers and told him thanks for being their teacher.

Not a bad day after all. Grace was also given her tape recorder back and her pistol with thanks. The recorder provided the whole story. Then Colonel Oakley stepped from behind the crowd. He came forward and shook Dan's hand. Then an unusual event took place. He presented Dan with the wings of a "bird" Colonel. Like Dan said, "Not a bad day".

The time is four months later. The attacks have stopped. Grace has had their baby, a beautiful little girl. The naming ceremony hadn't taken place yet as Grace had to get over the shock of shooting a man. She had to go through the ordeal of the hearing. The Colonel had sent a couple of special lawyers to side with Grace for the hearing.

The judge here had heard of what happened and the judge didn't want to be made to look like a fool in front of his local people. So, he didn't fight their plea of self-defense more than was prudent and adequate to show he was protecting his own. The judge wound up announcing a verdict of self-defense.

Dan and Grace had gotten over the changes and were at peace. At least they were when they were allowed to sleep. Grace was holding up quite nicely with the baby's feeding schedule. A schedule much different than that of almost any adult. But they were totally smitten with her and she had both of them wrapped around her little finger.

The time was nearly there in which they were going to drive over to Alder Grove and bless their little girl in the church with Grace's family. Church started at 10:00 on Sunday so they had to leave by 9:00 to make it in time. The timing wasn't too bad for the little one's schedule, but you never know when Murphy's Law will come into play. With luck, they should be there in time.

When they arrived at the church, the parking lot was almost full. It looked like half of the population of Cleaveland was there. The Chief of Police, Josh Parker, Helmut and Gretta Schmidt, the deputy sheriff, and also a major contingent from Dan's school. Dan's ROTC class was there in uniform and many other students, staff and the president.

Dan was in full uniform. Then to their surprise, Colonel Oakley was there and the Lieutenant Governor. The bishop was flabbergasted. We will fill the entire building. It was good for Dan and Grace to see our friends. It was a joyful reunion and many people were glad to meet so many others.

After all of the quick reunions and introductions, they moved into the chapel. There were so many they had to open up the folding doors into the overflow area and set up folding chairs.

After the opening exercise, the bishop called for Daniel Jorgensen to bring his little daughter up front to be blessed. Bishop Herndon told the congregation that the little girl's name would be Helen Jorgensen. Those who were asked to participate in the blessing were to come forward at this time. Six men in total, including Dan and the bishop, Helen's grandfather, stood in the circle. Dan gave Helen her name and then did something unusual. He asked Grace's father, Bishop Herndon, to pronounce a blessing upon Helen. He seemed grateful and emotional at this opportunity, to bless his first grandchild.

After the sacrament service, many of Dan and Grace's friends started to leave. Helmut spoke up and invited all who wanted to come to the lodge in Cleaveland were welcome. There was a dinner on the house. Grace told her parents they were going to the lodge and would come back to visit after the dinner.

The dinner at the lodge was fantastic and boisterous. It lasted a couple of hours. People began to leave with many well wishes. Colonel Oakley, CIE commander, asked Dan if he would be willing to return as the deputy commander. Dan told him, "It is a tempting offer, but I have found my place. Now that "Bobby" is out of the way it is quiet here. Besides, I'm training a new group of CIE candidates for you ".

The goodbyes with Helmut and Gretta were subdued and tearful, but Dan told them they would see him and his family again, soon. Dan, Grace and Helen then went to the Herndon's. It was a pleasant reunion without a crowd. Grace's father had one question that he was anxious to ask them "Where did the name Helen come from?"

Grace then explained that the name Helen was at her wish. "It is the name of Dan's first wife that was killed in London by a buzz bomb during the war. She died just about three months after they were married. Dan's memory of her was such that Dan could never look at a woman, until I came into his life. She saved Dan for me ".

CHAPTER NINE
A Peaceful Life

Daniel Jorgensen, Colonel, is now a teacher at Knoxville College, Knoxville, Colorado. It is now mid-August 1957. The college is a liberal arts college with an enrollment of around 5,400 students.

Knoxville is a town of about 9000 population, nestled in a rather wide verdant canyon on the west side of the Rocky Mountains. The mountains, toward the northeast and southeast of the end of the canyon, rose to 10,000 and 11,000 feet.

The green of the of the area being due to the pines and spruce trees that pretty well covered the mountains. Down in the flat land a number of maples filled in among the evergreen trees. It is now September. In the fall the maples turned a vibrant orange or red. In the upper reaches of the mountains, below the tree line, quaking aspen trees were found in patches. These patches of trees were a lighter green than the evergreen trees during the summer and turned golden yellow in the fall. With the yellow of the aspen trees, the green of the evergreens and the red and oranges of the maples during the fall it presented a colorful patchwork collage that surrounded the town. It is a sight to behold, and one to remember.

The patches of aspen could each be a group of trees that are all extensions from a single tree's roots. The roots spread from the "mother" tree. New trees will sprout up from the roots of the mother tree at set intervals from the original tree. So, each patch may actually be one individual tree with many parts. He decided that this is one item he could teach in his biology classes.

Dan and his wife have been here now nearly a year and a half and it is now early September. He was now in his office preparing a lesson for his biology class. Now, even with his degree as Doctor of Veterinary Medicine under his belt, he has to do a lot of review to keep up and a little ahead of his biology class. That is not a burden for him because while he is learning, he is mentally alive. He loves this job like he has never loved his work before. However, being a meat inspector for the army during World War II for a couple of years and then as an investigator for the Criminal Investigation Element (CIE) of the Army for eight more years didn't test his mental capabilities quite like this job. The CIE assignment was a real taxing job and sometimes a dangerous one. But this teaching job, which tested his mental capacity, kept him alive.

His transition from CIE to being a teacher had been fraught with dangers. There had been several attempts on his life and that of his beautiful and wonderful wife. He had been shot, shot at several times, an attempt to run him over by a pickup truck, an attempt at killing him and his wife by ramming them with a sports utility vehicle, a fake anthrax scare, and at least three attempts by bombs. The attempts on their lives had nothing to do with the teaching job, however it did tend to show Dan that he had been up as a target in a shooting gallery. This kept him on his toes…

As Grace was no longer a police officer and had occasion to need a weapon for defense of herself and me, she had a need to legally be able to carry a weapon at all times. Since the CIE considered me to be rather important, we were able to obtain a commission as a first lieutenant for Grace and the position as an auxiliary CIE officer, which required that Grace carry a weapon. At times she is required to wear a uniform with a sidearm, loaded. It was comforting to me to know she had her revolver for her protection, which she preferred over the army Colt 45 regulation pistol. It was and is a comfort to me to know of the skill, speed and accuracy Grace has with her 38 special revolvers

This job may not be of an exciting nature like the CIE was, if you ignore the attempts on my life, nor does it pay quite the same. But he would not go back to the CIE for love nor money. He appreciated the offer he had received to go back to the CIE as deputy commander, but he had turned it down. Here he had peace, contentment and love. Love big time with his wife whom he dearly loved and our angel of a daughter. An expression came to mind, "*Not for love nor war*". Dan had too much to do with war, war against the vilest of humanity.

Here he had the opportunity to battle the war against stupidity and ignorance. Stupidity, and that brought to mind another memory. "*The two most abundant things in the universe are hydrogen and helium and the two most abundant things on earth are hydrogen and stupidity*". Dan thought that hopefully he might be able to reduce the abundance of the stupidity, even if only a little bit. He hoped to be able to teach his students how to think and make considered decisions.

An hour later Dan had finished what he wanted to prepare about the Q10 concept and its meaning. This is one of the most important concepts in the study of biology and for that matter, almost every field of science. The Q10 temperature coefficient is a measure of the change of a biological or chemical system reaction rate as a consequence of increasing, or decreasing, the temperature. A reaction rate is doubled if the temperature of the system is raised by 10 °C, or cut in half if the temperature is lowered by 10 °C. This change of reaction rate is true up to a certain point. Beyond the given points, high or low, death usually follows rather quickly.

Then he spent a short time reviewing the progress of the students of the self-defense class and what to go over in their next session. That was always a question, what to teach the students in their next class. The class was progressing quite well and had covered nearly all of the basic procedures necessary to defend one's self. Perhaps today I could have the class go through the maneuvers they had already learned, one after the other as a review. A review and a reminder of what they should know and be able to do automatically if attacked.

Dan would review his plans for the ROTC class after lunch. This group of students was also doing well. Except David. He seemed to be bright enough but he was clumsy and it was as if he had only thumbs, and they were not coordinated. But his biggest problem was his lack of self-confidence. "What can I do to help him with that problem? If I can help him with that, it will be worth more than all of the other tasks of life". Dan continued contemplating David and his problem when a knock at the door pulled him out of his mental activity and anguish.

Dan spoke out rather loudly in order to be heard, "Come in."

The President of the school came in. He had a frown on his face, furrows on his brow and the look of great concern. When he spoke, his speech had the quality of reluctance to speak but seemed forced to do so. He slowly said, and quietly, "I am sorry to disturb you but I have a serious problem which I hope you can help me with. Someone has apparently embezzled about $100,000 and our comptroller has disappeared. We don't want to report this until it is absolutely necessary. With your experience as an investigator, I figured you might be able to help me. Could you or would you do that? Would you help me?"

Dan replied, "I would be glad to try and help you. $100,000 is a pretty great sum and it could have devastating effects on this school. I like it here and I don't want the school to have such a problem. I will need to talk with your accountant and I will need access to the financial records. An independent auditor will also be necessary. ""We already have such an auditor on hand and he is here right now. As soon as you can free yourself, I will take you to them. I can 't thank you enough."

Dan thought for a few seconds and told the President, "If you could wait a couple of minutes, I could free myself and then be able to go with you. Then we will see if I can be of help." President Wilson (no relation to Woodrow Wilson) said, "By all means, this is of utmost importance".

Dan finished what he had been doing and followed President Wilson to the accounting office. When they entered, the accountant and the auditor looked up in surprise. Their expressions quickly changed to anger and the auditor asked, "Why are you bringing your ROTC teacher in here? There is confidential and critical information in here!"

The President told them, "This is Colonel Dan Jorgensen of the CIE, or maybe in case this does not mean anything to you, the Criminal Investigation Element of the Army. He was their chief investigator. He has top secret security clearance and is probably the foremost investigator in the nation. I have asked him to help figure out this dilemma and I instruct you to give him whatever help or information he requests ".

They frowned and were slow in their indication of agreement to comply with the president's orders; it surely looked like this was not to their liking. They obviously were not happy to let an outsider enter into their domain. Is this totally territorial jealousy, he thought, or is there another reason for their reluctance to allowing me into their private kingdom? Are they covering up something that would not be to their advantage? We will see and if this is the case then let them squirm.

Dan sat down and asked them, "Will you show me the entries that you have found which show the embezzlement of $100,000? If you have found $100,000 missing, it is my guess that what you have found is the tip of the ice berg. Show me what you have found and then let me look at the books. I have encountered this type of situation before and such cases that involved millions of dollars ". They looked to the President and he nodded his head.

With reluctance they handed Dan the books. Dan began an amazingly rapid search of the financial documents. He quickly found that at least $175,000 was missing. He then showed the accountant and auditor the entries that contained the additional losses. They were startled and wondered how this ROTC instructor could surpass themselves, professional accountants, in finding records of missing money. Dan told them, "It is quite simple and before this is finished, I will show you how this is done." There were more books to go over, but the accountant and auditor could fill in the gaps, as soon as he was able to instruct them as to what they were to look for. Which he did to their amazement. That didn't take long.

Then Dan asked to see the office of the missing comptroller. The accountant and the auditor looked rather foolish as Dan left, like boys that has been found with their hands in the cookie jar. And what a cookie jar! Had they actually had their hands in this cookie jar? Were they both embezzlers and afraid that Dan would find evidence and show that they were the guilty parties? Time will tell.

Dan was taken into the office of the missing comptroller. His office was rather large and was much like a small library. The books were often a favorite place to hide information, in the case of the comptroller, financial records he didn't want others to see. So, this is where he began his search with a perusal of the books in the office. Every few minutes he would pull down a book and look it over rather closely. After Dan had looked at several books, he told the President, "With a court order, I think we can recover about $150,000. But we will need a bit more data to support such a request of the court. Give me about an hour and I may be able to find the evidence for that and probably more. Also, I think I can put my finger on the guilty person, someone other than the comptroller ".

The president's relief was almost palpable. Dan then told President Wilson, "If my guess is correct. The comptroller is not the one that caused this criminal action. I believe he was being forced to do this stealing to protect one or more members of his family from bodily harm and shame. The latter can be just as harmful as physical damage. Sir we need to report this in order to obtain court orders to save as much of the money and as quickly as possible before the money is moved out of our reach. Also, to obtain information that will lead us to the actual criminals guilty of this crime ".

So, at the president's nod of agreement and request to proceed, Dan began to search and compile data to show how much money had been stolen and where most of the money was. He also made notes which he hoped would lead to the guilty party or parties. Dan also had a hunch that the comptroller was dead. The court orders would help to locate the comptroller, dead or alive.

The court orders were obtained in two days. Dan took his senior ROTC class with him out to the residence of the comptroller. He told the students to wear their uniforms and he instructed them what to look for. The search party included a couple of deputies from the sheriff's office along with Dan, Dan's ROTC students and the deputies were to provide some supervision and instructions for the ROTC students about this search, search procedures and precautions. The deputies were to handle any evidence found, in order to make sure the handling of the evidence was done properly, so it would be admissible in court.

One item they searched for was the body of the comptroller. His instructions were that if they came across anything suspicious, they were to back off and go no further and inform me, or one of the deputies. I or a deputy would complete the necessary search. I didn't want the students to actually find a dead body.

The comptroller's home and property were a bit out from the edge of town and it occupied several acres of land, part of it was forest, some pasture and a small orchard. A fantastic and beautiful setting. A person that loved to grow things could love this place. There was a barn and a few other outbuildings. Dan sent the students out in pairs with the instructions to not touch anything. If they saw anything or, heaven forbid, if they smelled something dead, they were to back away and notify me or one of the deputies. Colonel Jorgensen, along with one deputy, did a thorough search of the home. The house looked like it hadn't been occupied for several days at least.

The deputy did a general search of the house which he did quite thoroughly and quickly. Dan focused on the library because that is one of the preferred spots of thieves and embezzlers to hide financial information. It didn't take long before Dan began to find what he was looking for. This would help the school recover a significant portion of their money. Dan continued looking for more information and made notes of his findings.

While this was going on, the students and the other deputy were about to finish a search of the farm buildings and land. Two students were approaching one of the last buildings, an old chicken coop. As they got near the building the stench, they encountered was horrible. They backed away as instructed and ran to find a deputy or the Colonel. They ran into a deputy quickly and they then lead him to the building. He looked in and then turned away, looking somewhat green around the gills so to speak. They walked away and the deputy went to his vehicle and called headquarters. He reported what was found and requested the coroner to come out. There was evidently no question as to what was found. They didn't have to look any further for the comptroller. This also confirmed part of Dan's theory.

The killer, or killers, must have been in a hurry. They had not buried the body of the comptroller. The body had probably been taken to the abandoned chicken coop and just left there, figuring they had time to make their escape.

The deputy that had been searching the house found a cache of money. There turned out to be about $35,000 stashed away. Dan found information that could lead to another $75,000. This accounts for an additional $110,000 of the school's finances in addition to the $175,000 recorded in the comptroller's office. The sheriff is going to have to act fast and get court orders to impound the moneys. The various deposits of money were in a variety of banks and credit bureaus. Some also in cash and certificates of deposits. There might even be some jewels or land. How long had this been going on? Well, they had just scratched the surface of the problem now, as far as Dan was concerned, the major problem was to find the one that caused the crime or sin, the one at the top of the heap of criminals.

This case now involved not just embezzlement, but also murder. Dan thought, well it looks like I'm in up to my neck all over again. Then Dan thought of something of something else, did the Comptroller have a family? If so then kidnapping must also be considered.

Freezing of the money in banks and credit bureaus would not be difficult and could be done rather quickly, which must be done pronto. Assets in the form of jewels and land would be harder to locate and require more time to be able to convert their values back to cash. Cash would be required in order for the school to be able to use these forms of assets. This will require more searches and court orders to find and recover the funds represented by any land or jewels. Once these assets were identified and located it would take some time to sell them and have the funds from their sales. Then the school would have back those usable assets.

CHAPTER TEN
It Has Started Again

Dan went to see the President and reported their findings. He was shocked when he found out that the comptroller was dead. Dan asked if the comptroller had a family, Pres. Wilson told him, "Yes, he did. He had a wife and a girl about ten years old and a younger boy. Are they missing too?"

"I'm afraid that they are but we need to check with family once they are identified. If you can give us any details about the comptroller's family it would be of great assistance."

"We can get at least some of the information you need from his personnel records. Follow me and we can have that information for you in a few minutes. At least the information we have on file. ". A review of the personnel records of the comptroller did not contain as much information as President Wilson thought.

The records didn't have information about the comptrollers' parents or siblings. The comptroller's name was Jerold Osgood but it did not contain any useful information to help with finding the comptroller 's family. So, Dan would have to find some alternate method of finding the critical information. Dan asked the ROTC students for help tracking down any Osgoods in the local area using local telephone directories. It turned out that there were quite a number of Osgood families listed in the phone books, so Dan assigned out the various listings to the students with the instructions to call each of the families and asking them about Jerold Osgood's family.

The students were rather active calling the various phone numbers, trying to find a family member related to Jerold Osgood. Most of the numbers called resulted in no answer, a few people that answered their phone calls were angry at the impertinent questions. But finally, bingo, the comptroller's father was located. Arrangements were made for Colonel Jorgensen to talk with Mr. Osgood so he could get information on his son's family.

It was delegated to Dan to inform the father of the death of his son. Also, Dan needed the information about his son's family. So, he went to see the former comptroller's father. Mr. Osgood was shocked when he heard of his son's death. After a minute or so to recover from the shock of this bad news, he told Dan about a sister of his son's wife. She often looked after the kids. And that was all he could think at the time. The death of his son had wiped out almost everything from his mind.

Dan apologized for the bad news and prepared to leave. Mr. Osgood told Dan, "I have been telling my son to get away from the crowd he was dealing with. I have been sure my son would get in deep trouble associating with that bunch of criminals, but I did not expect this. I'm sorry, but I can't give you any information about those people my son was mixed up with ".

Dan's next stop was to Mrs. Osgood's sister's home. When he arrived, he found Mrs. Osgood in residence there. Dan told her that he had some bad news for her. He then told her of finding her husband's body. She broke down and collapsed to the ground. Her sister came quickly to look after her. Dan asked if the children were here and found they were. It was a relief that they were. Then Dan told them he would ask the sheriff to provide some surveillance for their protection. Dan said he would need to ask some questions later as they needed some information about her husbands associates. Dan then departed to let Mrs. Osgood mourn in peace, if that were possible.

Dan then went to the sheriff's office to report to the sheriff. The sheriff was appalled at the death of Jerold Osgood and the theft of over one quarter of a million dollars from the college. He also appreciated the assistance Dan was giving his department and approved Dan's continued involvement in this case. This was expected because the efforts of Colonel Jorgensen and his students produced good results, and this without time or expense to the sheriff's office. This made for good reports to the county commissioners to his benefit.

We can now eliminate kidnapping as a possible charge. One question in Dan's mind was, why were the wife and children staying with her sister? It was obvious that they had been there longer than just a few days. Probably longer than the comptroller had been dead. Why? My guess is that Mr. Osgood suspected some trouble and danger for he and his family and moved his family out of what he considered the danger zone. He had done this none too soon. It's too bad he hadn't moved himself out of harm's way at the same time. No chance of that now, at least in mortality. He was out of the criminals' reach now. Dan thought about this situation over the next day and realized that it has started again. Maybe I'll not tell Grace about this one just yet. No need to worry her. The time will come soon enough when I will have to tell Grace about this new investigation.

Dan had reported their findings to Pres. Wilson and the probability of recovering more of the missing money. The president was pleased with the results of what Dan had done thus far, but was saddened by the death of their comptroller, Jerold Osgood. Dan continued compiling information about where money was and how much. The list is as follows:

Local bank -	$55,000
Bank 1	$75.050
Bank 2	$25,100
College Credit Union	$15,250
Cash found	$35,000
TOTAL	$205,400

This left about $81,000 unaccounted for, if my previous figures were correct. This money could be in jewels or land. This will require more intensive searches to identify and locate. The immediate task is to obtain a court order to freeze this money and get it returned to the school. This could save President Wilson's position at the college. This money had been siphoned off over the last six months, and that was a very large amount during such a short period of time. Questions would be asked by the board of governors of the school how this could take place without being detected. How could this have happened? What could the school do to prevent this ever happening again? Probably a new accountant, auditor and comptroller to start.

The application of the court orders resulted in the recovery of $197,000, including the cash found. The loss of $8,400 while not a loss to be sneezed at, was nothing compared to the funds recovered. And this did not include the $81,000 left unaccounted for. Who was, or who were responsible for the loss?

Dan began looking over the entries associated with the loss. They were nearly all related to a construction project or the supplies for construction. Dan sought the president and asked about construction projects over the last six to nine months. There had been three such projects and who knows how many suppliers were involved. Dan began to look at the suppliers listed. Several names were listed, but something looked fishy. One company could have a physical address a couple of times and a post office box for others, not all the same town and not all the same PO Box number. Other suppliers had the same PO Box number in the same town. This was a convoluted arrangement. One designed to fool a casual auditor or a preliminary audit. Cleaver! Based on this finding of the entries I have seen; I would watch all contractor fees and charges for supplies. This as an added precaution to prevent such loss in the future.

Dan had his ROTC students look through telephone directories looking for suppliers found in the school's invoices and a search in the phone books for suppliers of the same name or addresses. The search came down to one supplier with three different addresses and three suppliers with the same address. Interesting. Dan talked with the sheriff about this and gave him a copy of their findings. When deputies went to the listed addresses, they found a mailing forwarding business. It took a court order, but they got what they hoped to be a real address. When they got there, it looked like the building had recently been vacated.

It looks like the mail forwarding business needs to be tracked as well. We didn't waste time getting here and yet they had even more quickly vacated the premises. And tracking down this fake construction material supplier could be interesting. A quick review of the vacated facility revealed a store of dummy products. An examination of the dummy products revealed a couple of partial names of possibly producer companies.

The first one was such:

        me Science Pr
        PO Box 47
        ME

        Item # 2-473-01

The second partial was:

This didn't give us much to start on, but something is better than nothing. This provided some more searching for my students. They may make CIE candidates yet. The surprising thing was that David tore into this and was able to cover about twice the search area of anyone else. He may not be a good possibility for CIE, but it looked like he would be a great intelligence analyst. And we need some of those, especially if they are good. David could be just that. He not only did a fast search, but it seemed to be thorough and came up with results.

The young men came up with the following companies that supplied some materials for the scam. The companies could be innocent suppliers but hopefully they could provide a lead for the receiver at this end.

The companies were:

Acme Science Products
P O Box 471
Portland, ME 04112-0471

Item No. 3473 - 01
Western Army Surplus
Kansas City, Kansas

This information was again turned over to the sheriff's office. A call to Colonel Oakley was made and a polite request for help about these two companies was made, The Colonel said, "That is no problem. Those two companies do not exist. The CIE has been working on the problem in which these two ghost companies have shown up a number of times." Dan proceeded to fill the Colonel in on the case here involving the school. Colonel Oakley said, "You had better act fast to recover the money, otherwise it would be out of the country."

I told him, "The court had already frozen these assets."

Well, it looks like we are back at square one, aside from

having the necessary information to recover most of the school's money, we had nowhere to turn at this time. All we can do is hope some information is gleaned from the records of the financial institutions where the school's money is being held.

It was the end of another day and Dan went home to his family. He would have to perk up because he did not want to take his troubles home. He also hoped that this problem doesn't spill over onto his family like the last one did. The best way to stop that was to find the guilty ones and put them behind bars. Dan also began to worry for the family of Jerold Osgood. They need to be given protection. If we could find them as easily as we did, the guilty ones can do it also. Dan would call the sheriff and see what they might be able to do. Dan spent a quiet evening with his family. After their little girl was put to bed, Grace joined him. She looked at Dan with a questioning and searching expression in her eyes. Then she asked, "Dan. What is wrong? Is something bothering you?"

Dan waited a moment or two before answering her. He knew there was no evading her inquiry. "There has been a great embezzlement at the school and the comptroller has been murdered. I am worried about the comptroller's family. I have found where most of the money is so the school shouldn't lose too much, but the murder is my biggest concern. I feel like the war has started all over again. I worry about you and Helen."

Grace then told me, "I can take care of myself and no one is going to get past me to get at Helen. I promise."

Dan took Grace into his arms and held her close. They spent quite some time like that. Just enjoying the touch of each other. An enlivening recharge. Dan loved Grace and Helen more than words can tell. More than life itself and he was not going to let this scum get at them. Come morning Dan would reassess this situation and talk with the sheriff. Some means of hiding the Osgood family would need to be found and carried out. The sooner the better.

Dan stopped by the sheriff's office first thing in the morning. He began telling the sheriff about hiding the Osgood family. The sheriff had a very sour expression on his face. "Too late. Mrs. Osgood's sister called late last night to tell us her sister and the children have disappeared. We can just hope they hid themselves and are hidden well. I also hope you can find some clue as to the identity of whoever is behind all of this, The FBI has been notified of the possible kidnapping of the Osgoods."

Dan went to work, he had some classes to prepare for and he should report to the President and bring him up to date. The President was waiting for him, a deep concern etched into his face. He looked at Dan and said, "I have been ordered to put you on suspension and tell you that you are to have nothing more to do with the investigation of the embezzlement of funds or the murder of Mr. Osgood. Your classes will be taken over by someone that should be okay with the students."

Dan looked at President Wilson and asked, "Who issued that order?"

The president answered, "I am not at liberty to say. For the time being, I would suggest you pick up your things and vacate the office."

When Dan got home, Grace was in tears. Mrs. Osgood's sister had come and screamed at her and said, "You led the criminals right to my sister ". She hollered at me and yelled at me for us to get out of town. The town has turned against us "

"Grace, I will take you to your family and then I'm getting to the bottom of this."

"No Dan don't leave me, even for a minute. I don't care where we go, but whatever you do, it will be with us together."

"Alright, but you make sure your sidearm is ready for action" as he strapped on his Colt 45. Grace replied, "It already is ready for action" as she pulled it out of her apron pocket.

"Okay, then we hang tight right here." Dan called the sheriff and talked with him. He already was aware of what was going on and he said his people would do what they could. Dan then called Colonel Oakley and brought him up to date. The Colonel dispatched four CIE staff members to Dan's assistance within the hour. They were coming in plain clothes this time rather than in military dress, and armed.

Dan decided to call his friend, John March the Lieutenant Governor, so he wouldn't be taken blindsided if something happened. Which it most likely would. John thanked him for the warning and asked Dan to keep him up to date. "When the time comes that you need help, whistle. Help would be on the way ".

Dan then called the sheriff again and told him of the developments. The sheriff said, "You do have friends in high places. Enemies as well. Keep your head down."

Dan and Grace then began their usual process of talking the problem through, trying to find the source of this harassment and the *"cause of the sin."*

Thinking back over the short history of this nightmare, the only ones that came to mind with any sort of antagonism against Dan, had been the accountant and the auditor at the school. The auditor evidently had just a short time of involvement with the school, after some indication of the embezzlement came to light. The accountant had been at the school for a few years. Both he and the auditor had been angry when Dan had been brought into the picture. Perhaps the accountant had called the attention to a short fall when the time for an audit was drawing close. If he brought up the problem it could direct suspicion away from him. He could have doctored the books to cover his trail and point the trail to the comptroller. Then I come along and redirects the suspicion from the comptroller to someone else. There weren't many others they could put the blame onto. This could be used to get rid of Colonel Jorgensen.

Since the FBI had been called in, Dan got hold of the FBI and asked to talk with the agent in charge. The agent didn't seem pleased or willing to talk with Dan. So, Dan took a different tack and got hold of Colonel Oakley again. The Colonel told him that the FBI believes that you are the source of the problem and won't listen to you, but I know you are not the problem. The Colonel gave Dan the authority he once had and ten men to help him with access to all CIE capability. Dan requested an investigation of the accountant, Ray Dawson, and the auditor, Leonard Anderson.

CHAPTER ELEVEN
The Battle is Joined

Dan went to talk with the sheriff. The sheriff was confused and didn't know who to believe. Dan laid it all out for the sheriff. The conclusions that he had figured out and why. Then he told the sheriff, "Think this over. What have I to gain? You can check all of my records, all transactions with banks or any financial institution and see that I have received nothing other than my wages. My wages from the US Army. I have received nothing from this college except the house they have given me to live in. I in turn have taught the biology class and the martial arts class with no other compensation. I took on the investigation of the embezzlement and subsequent discovery of the murder of the comptroller at no cost to the school at the request of President Wilson. And for what? I have been driven out. They've taken my teaching post away. I have to leave the home I was given. I don't know where we are going to live. But we will make it. In spite of this, I will help you all I can."

"I appreciate that and I will look into what you have told me. I hope we can get to the bottom of this. We need you here, even if some misguided people don't think that. When you are cleared, will you come back here and teach? I certainly hope you do because from what I 've heard, you are quite some wizards of a teacher"

"I haven't decided that yet. This will take some serious consideration. I don't take kindly to these people turning on me with no evidence. Just some gossip to base their opinions on. With friends like that I don't need any enemies."

"I have about come to that same conclusion a number of times myself. The public is so fickle. You're their hero one day, their villain the next and their scapegoat all of the time. Good luck and let me know when you are settled. How are you doing financially?"

"We're doing okay in that regard. I have been reinstated in the CIE in full capacity and given a number of investigators to assist me. This problem at the school is only the tip of the iceberg that is affecting the Army as well. I will work on that angle. If the two paths cross, so much the better. I believe Victor Hugo when he said, *"the guilty one is the one that caused the sin."*

"Good Luck Colonel Jorgensen."

With that, I packed up my family and prepared to move to Quantico, VA. President Wilson saw us preparing to move and stopped by, "You're leaving? I didn't mean you had to leave."

"I'm afraid that is what it sounded like to me. I no longer have a job here and this home was provided for me as a teacher here at this school. You dismissed me so I have no job and therefore I have no claim on this house. Everyone, including you, have turned against me. I don't like fair weather friends which is just what you are. So, we are leaving."

"Will you come back?"

"Right now, I doubt it. As I told you before, I don't care for fair weather friends. I was putting my heart into this job, I liked what I was doing. I thought I was actually helping some of these students. And look what happened. How can I trust you and these people? The sheriff seems to be the only one willing to give me a chance. Goodbye."

I turned my back on him and walked away. About that time five ROTC cadets showed up. Not in uniform. They looked at me with anger in their faces. "You're leaving us just like that?" And their voices dripped with hostility. Their attitudes pleased me in a way, yet they also disturbed me greatly. They had made a hasty decision without obtaining any further information.

I told them, "You need to hear and understand my response to your reaction to my leaving. You have made a decision without acquiring information which would be needed in order to be able to evaluate the truth. I ask you, what am I to do? I have been dismissed. As a result of my dismissal, I have been recalled to the CIE. There I know who my friends are and who my enemies are. That is life. You have heads on your shoulders. Hold them high and keep fighting for what is right. I am continuing this fight from another direction. I intend to bring this scum down. I don't want you to be in the danger of this action. You will have plenty of time for that later. Good luck my friends."

They saluted and turned away. This was one of the hardest times that I have had to face. One does not like these times. But they happen in life and we have to learn to accept what comes and how to cope with them Perhaps we will meet again.

We continued packing up and were ready to leave when a car pulled up in front. Two men and a woman got out of the car and marched up to me with stern looks on their faces. "You are leaving? "They asked with less than friendly tones in their voices.

"And who are you?" I replied.

"We are three members of the board of governors. I'm George Wilcox, Chairman, this is Waren Englehart, and Amelia Roland. Why are you leaving?"

I considered their question and apparent attitude, thinking that the school president had not informed them of the current situation. "President Wilson suspended me and as a result of that I have been ordered to return to Quantico, the CIE headquarters. I have no alternative. If the president hadn't suspended me, I could have stayed on. But with the suspension the CIE had no alternative but to recall me. There is nothing we can do. I'm sorry to be leaving, but that is out of my hands. I thought I was helping some of my students to learn how to think and make informed decisions rather than making decisions based on whims. I enjoyed that, and my ROTC student, David, I believe was beginning to gain in self-confidence. That is his biggest problem. If he can develop confidence in himself, he can have a great career in intelligence analysis. He has a knack for that. We don't need to tell the students what they are to become, we just need to help them find out that for themselves ".

"The normal process in teaching students is to mold them into a common rut with no sense of thinking out of the box. Those who do think out of the box are the ones that give all of us the greatest gain and improvements. I'm sorry Ma'am and gentlemen. But there is nothing more I can do. I only wish there were and I have a mandated time for complying to my current orders. I'm sorry that I must be on my way. Good day."

They left with their faces down turned and sour. I suspect that President Wilson is going to have his ears bent. I am sure he won't appreciate that and wish he hadn't suspended me. Too late now.

Grace and I weren't happy with the turn of events as we were going to need a new home. They weren't always easy to find, even on a military base.

We were ready for the long drive to Virginia. We were loaded up and started to drive away when a car pulled up in front of me. It was a telegraph delivery person and he handed me a sealed envelope and requested my signature. I signed and took the telegram. The message was in code. I had to get out my code book to decipher the message.

I couldn't believe my eyes. We were not going to Virginia; we were to go to Peterson Field near Colorado Springs for transportation to a destination we would be informed of at the air base. So, off we go into the wild blue unknown with Grace driving our car and me at the wheel of our rented truck. Peterson is nearer than Virginia by about eighteen hours. I wonder where we are being sent now.

We arrived at Peterson Field and stopped at the main entrance gate. A Senior Airman came to my window and I showed him my orders. He read the orders and smiled. Then said, "You will be escorted to the Commander's office for your special orders." That's strange. An Airman pulled out in a security police car and motioned for us to follow. He took us in a crazy, mind-boggling route, not to the command building but into a big hangar. Once inside the hanger, we were directed to park our vehicles in an area obscured from the outside. Then a master sergeant pulled alongside of us in an Air Force blue van and asked us to get in. Then he took us to the Security Police headquarters and escorted us into the building and into an interrogating room.

I asked, "What is going on?"

The sergeant said, "I don't know sir."

Then the wing commander came into the room. He was a colonel. I saluted him and reported to him and asked for instructions or orders. The colonel looked at me with a queer expression on his face. "Either you are one hell of an important person or else in real trouble. I have never seen anything like your orders before. Here they are. Read them and then they will be destroyed. There is supposed to be no record of what is being done." He looked at me quizzically and said, "On second thought, you wouldn't be getting this treatment for being in trouble unless you were important. Colonels make as good of bomb fodder as many, and more than others. "

He then handed me my orders. I read them and showed Grace. She read them and then looked at me with her eyes as big as saucer plates and shock on her face.

"What does this mean Dan?"

"I wish I knew."

The Colonel then shook our hands and told us, "Good luck." I saluted him and he turned and left the room. Then another sergeant came in carrying a different uniform, an Army uniform with captain's bars on the shoulders. The name tag read Edward Higgens. He also gave me a new set of orders. The sergeant then handed Grace a sheet of instructions and ID papers. The sergeant looked at me and asked, "Excuse me sir, but who are you anyway?" I quickly glanced at my orders and answered him, "Captain Edward Higgens, US Army." I was shown into another room where I changed into my new uniform. I was now Capt. Edward Higgens and I knew nothing about myself. What have I gotten into this time? What am I supposed to do? The only thing I knew was that I am now supposed to report to the commander of Fort Carson, just a few miles away.

I came out where Grace and Helen were waiting for me. Grace looked like she was a little frightened, because she didn't know what was going on. But then neither did I. The sergeant then handed me a sealed envelope with instructions to open only when in the commander's office at Fort Carson. He also handed me another envelope with my new driver's license and assorted papers pertaining to my new identification and a set of car keys.

We were then taken out to where our car and truck were. But they were gone and a new car was in their place. Not brand new, but new to us. It even looked a bit used and had the personal items of Helen's and Grace inside on the seats. Except there were no indications of our former names.

The sergeant then handed me a map that would lead me to Fort Carson. He shook my hand and saluted. "Good luck sir."

Now we were off again. Into what? I wish I knew.

We climbed into the car and we were escorted back to the main gate. The sergeant saluted as we left the gate. Grace acted as my navigator as I headed for Fort Carson. She was a good navigator and this made the drive to the Fort simple and without any complications.

At the main gate of Fort Carson, I stopped and rolled down my window. A lieutenant stood at the side of my car and looked in and viewed all present. He asked for my ID and orders. I told him I was to open my orders only in the presence of the commander. The lieutenant said, "Will you pull into that parking spot sir? "He then indicated that I pull into a parking spot, pointing to one, and instructed me, "Wait there ". The lieutenant went into the guard post and made a phone call. A sergeant then came out and instructed me to follow him. He escorted me to the commander's office. He left me only when a major in the commander's office relieved the sergeant of responsibility for us.

The major asked to see my orders. I repeated my instructions to him and refused to release or open them. He got angry and ordered me to hand my orders over to him. I repeated my instructions and said, "If you cannot accept the instructions I have received, I suggest you talk to your commander or else call the commander of the CIE at Quantico." The major got a shocked look on his face at this and asked, "Who are you? "I said, "Captain Edward Higgens, US Army." You know, this is getting a bit out of hand I thought. I wish I knew what was going on.

About this time, the Commander, Major General Lewis Warner came out of his office. He looked a bit confused at first and then his face brightened up and asked, "Captain, are you Edward Higgens?" "Yes sir," I said. The general turned to the major and told him "It is okay. I will take them from here ". He spoke to the major under his breath, "By the way, this man out ranks you and I wonder if I should be saluting him myself." At this the major really looked shocked and surprised. He didn't know what to say.

The General opened his office door and indicated that I and my family were to enter, which we did. He then closed the door on the major's totally lost and confused expression, and offered us seats. The General looked at me for a moment and then said, "Colonel, you lead an interesting and exciting life. Mrs. Jorgensen, yours doesn't seem much less exciting. Myself I prefer things a bit more peaceful."

Grace said, "Sir, we do too. But that isn't the deck of cards we have been dealt from. We seem to be the moving target of a group of professional killers. It isn't the least bit fun or peaceful."

"I don't doubt that in the least. Colonel, will you open your orders now? I think that I am about as curious to find out what is going on and what you are to do as you both are. So, if you please, go ahead and open them."

I opened the envelope and pulled out the sheaf of papers. I began reading and then I was shocked beyond anything I had received before. I asked the General, "Are you sure you want to hear this? I would rather something different but I can't change them. These orders are issued over the signature of our Commander in Chief, President Dwight David Eisenhower".

The General leaped out of his chair and came around his desk to see my orders. The color drained from his face. He sputtered, "I have never seen such orders before nor the signature of the President." The General returned to his seat and looked at me with a bit of fear evident. "Why are you here?"

I told him, "I know no more about this than what you have seen, Sir. Perhaps we need to read the rest of these orders." Dan turned to Grace and told her, "I have been promoted to Brigadier General and made commander of the CIE. I wish I knew what was going on".

Dan continued reading his orders for the benefit of all present. Colonel Oakley had been murdered. Before his death he had recommended me to be the CIE commander. Due to circumstances, the CIE headquarters was being temporarily transferred to Fort Carson. Fort Carson was one of the most secure bases in the country, especially with Peterson Field nearby. This would reduce security problems for me. I would answer only to the Army Chief of Staff, the Secretary of Defense or the President of the United States.

So now we had our real identifications back and would be living on Fort Carson. This caused no small problem for General Warner. I apologized to him for this and he replied, "Those orders are from our Commander in Chief for both of us. We can only carry out those orders. We will provide temporary housing in the visitor quarters and have a home for you, hopefully within a week. An office and staff that is another problem. I believe that the Post Police Headquarters can provide you an office for the time being."

Dan then noticed a smaller envelope in with his orders, one that was a bit more bulky. He opened it and inside were his ID for his shirt and his stars, plus instructions to put them on immediately. Dan had Grace apply the stars with the General's help. The General still seemed a bit reluctant to look at Dan. General Warner out ranked Dan, but the position of CIE commander was rather intimidating to any in the army. After the changes were complete, General Warner said, "I will have the major take you and your family, first to the Post Exchange so you can acquire the necessary items needed for your rank and position. Then the major would take you to the visitor quarters ".

They left the General's office and when the major saw the stars on Dan's uniform, his face suddenly paled. The major then noticed Dan's command insignia, CIE and almost fainted. The General smiled at this response. Dan was kind of looking forward to meeting the lieutenant from the guard post and seeing his response. The reaction of the Post Exchange personnel was also interesting, but courteous and quick. When they arrived at the visitor quarters Dan saw a car parked there with plates showing one star. The General acted pretty fast.

After they were at least temporarily settled in their quarters, they had lunch at the Officer's Club. The reactions at the club were about as expected. Word of Dan's presence on the Post and his rank and office spread like wild fire.

After they had eaten, Dan took Grace and Helen back to the visitor quarters. Then Dan went to the Security Police station to check where his office would be.

He walked into the building, everyone jumped to attention. Their Commander, Colonel Schnell approached him, saluted and welcomed him to their facilities. Colonel Schnell offered Dan his own office, but Dan refused. He told the Colonel, "The security of this post is even more critical now than it was at the beginning of this day. I don't want anything to interfere with the operation of this unit. The moving of your office would cause such an interference. I have had too many attempts against my life, which almost reached an end while on Quantico. I would prefer to be safe in the hands of a competent Security Police organization". The Colonel and his staff stood a little taller and straighter following my words.

Dan had demonstrated one principle of command with respect. If you respect your people, they will respect you. Dan acknowledged the position of Colonel Schnell and these actions had made Colonel Schnell's position here at Fort Carson in a more solid and concrete status. This also placed Dan on more firm footing with the security police here at Fort Carson. And Dan's life depends on them in more ways than one.

Dan was given an office in the Security Police headquarters and was at least in a space for himself. He had a desk, a chair and a telephone. But what was he to do? That was the main item on his mind. As he sat there thinking this situation over, his phone rang. He answered, "General Jorgensen here."

"Well general, this is General Crane, Chief of Staff. How are you doing?"

"Lost. I don't know how I ended up here in this position. I don't know what I am to do nor where to start. I have no information about the current situation with the CIE nor any staff. What do you want me to do Sir? What are my orders?"

"Well first of all, I want you here at the Pentagon for a couple of days. We will have everything you need shipped to Fort Carson. What can be left at Quantico, records, files and people, let's leave them there. When you are here, we can discuss what to send to Fort Carson plus what and whom to leave back here. A plane will be ready at 0700 hours tomorrow morning to bring you here to Andrews AFB or to Quantico where a helicopter will bring you to the Pentagon. Send a message to Colonel Johnson at Quantico, your deputy, and have at least four CIE personnel sent to Fort Carson to assist you now. Glad to have you on board Dan. Till tomorrow. Goodbye."

Well, I know a little bit more than I did an hour ago. But not enough to keep out of trouble. Dan left and went to the visitor quarters. When he tried to enter, a security policeman stopped him. Then realizing who Dan was stepped back, saluted and let him enter, saying, "Good afternoon, Sir." Dan thought, boy life can get complicated in a hurry. The more he thought about this whole problem, the more it looked like a large organization was involved again. Am I a giant mob magnet that I can pull them into my life? This is so unreal. But the bullets have been real.

Dan entered their temporary quarters and talked with Grace. She wasn't happy that I was going to be gone for a couple of days but I assured her that she and Helen would be okay. Dan certainly hoped so. Grace had her pistol and would not let anyone into their suite. They had adequate food and milk. They would be okay.

But, both of us had a restless night. The idea of being separated for even two days was not fun or pleasant at all. It reminded them of the time just four days after they were married when Dan had been arrested and spent four days in jail under false charges of attempted murder. Those days of separation were not enjoyable and they were not looking forward to Dan being gone.

CHAPTER TWELVE
What is My Task

At 0650 hours, Dan was at the air terminal at Peterson Field for his flight to Andrews AFB. The Senior Airman that checked him in the day before checked him in today. He about went into shock when he saw Dan as a brigadier general when he had been a colonel before. The Senior Airman said, "You sure get fast promotions."

And I responded, "That's what you get for living in the fast and dangerous lane." With that, he waved me through.

I thought about the airman's comment about my fast promotions and I remembered the history of the promotions of President Dwight Eisenhower. President Eisenhower went from Lieutenant Colonel to General of the Army (a five-star rank) in 3 years and nine months. That was a promotion about every 7½ months. I have gone from lieutenant colonel to brigadier general in 1 year and 4 months (16 months).

The pilot of my flight was waiting for me. He saw my rank and insignia and got a little less colorful, but he remained composed. He asked an airman to take my baggage who stopped when he saw that it was handcuffed to my wrist. They both shrugged and the pilot told me to follow him. We went out to the parking apron; the morning was still dark and very cold. This could be expected in September of 1958 at an altitude close to one mile high. A skiff of snow had fallen during the night. With the altitude and being on the east side of the Rockies, Peterson Field often got some unpleasant weather. We got aboard a twin engine airplane. Dan was astonished when he saw that he was the only passenger. This caused him to be a bit uncomfortable but there was nothing he could do about that. Dan took a seat and buckled in. He certainly hoped this flight wouldn't take long and would be a smooth one. I was hoping for a quick take off but due to the cold and the light snow that had fallen we had to be deiced before we could take off. That didn't take as long as I thought it would.

The plane took off shortly.

We had a fairly good tail wind so the flight only took five and a half hours instead of the predicted six hours. They arrived about 1530 hours (that is 3:30 pm) eastern time. On deplaning, Dan was directed to a helicopter nearby and he was off in the Marine helicopter in fifteen minutes. They arrived at the Pentagon about fifteen minutes later. He was escorted to the Army staff offices and then immediately ushered into the office of the Army Chief of Staff. He was glad for a guide because the Pentagon was a most confusing building inside, being five rings inside one another with what seems no apparent rhyme nor reason for the numbered locations in the building. I wonder what it would have been like had they completed this building as a hospital. It was built in preparation for the anticipated 1,000,000 casualties if they attacked the Japanese home land towards the end of World War two. Dan had been here before but that didn't reduce his confusion any at all.

General Crane welcomed Dan into his office and closed the door. The General started immediately instructing him on what he was expected to accomplish. "Colonel Oakley had been tortured before his death. He had been tortured unmercifully for some time. The killer or killers figured he was dead and left him as if dead. He lived about fifteen to twenty minutes after he was found. He was unable to tell those who found him who the attackers were. They were masked. They wanted to know where you were. He didn't tell them. At least we're pretty sure he didn't tell them."

"Colonel Oakley told his rescuers that you were to be CIE commander. So, you are the commander. Since there was a near fatal attack on you at Quantico, we figured you needed to be set up somewhere else. We chose Fort Carson. This has caused General Warner considerable work to make accommodations for you, and the staff you're going to need. Well, he will be given what resources he needs to accomplish that. Let him work it out. He is a good man."

"Dan, your job is to protect yourself, your family and find Colonel Oakley's killers. You will be given full support. The murder of Colonel Oakley is considered as a national security issue. The murder of the Colonel is to be your number two priority, with the safety and protection of you and your family being your number one priority."

Dan thought for a few minutes and then told General Crane, "Sir, the key to this entire series of events is at Knoxville College, Knoxville, Colorado. The key being involved with the death of the college's comptroller and the embezzlement of over $250,000. This case has started to unravel a nationwide system of theft and murder. Also, there is a high likelihood of kidnapping of the Osgood family children. The FBI was called in on that case and the school turned against me. I am sure that I need to go back there and stir the fire a bit more. I feel that will bring the rats out of their holes where we can pick them off. I also have a hunch as to one of the kingpins of that whole operation, the operation of the gang that killed Colonel Oakley, my dear friend and benefactor. Sir, I request approval to start this ball rolling."

"That sounds reasonable, but do you need to be the one to set yourself up as the target? For that is exactly what you would be doing."

"Hiding in the past hasn't protected me. It nearly got me killed. Hiding this time has gotten Colonel Oakley killed, the commander of CIE. He was a good, capable man, commander and friend. If I stay in my hole now, who is going to be the next person to die in their attempt to get at me? Quantico was not secure enough to protect me. Is Fort Carson secure enough to protect me or my family? I really don't think so. The motto of the CIE is, *"Do what has to be done."* I also remember something else I have learned in the Army, *"The best defense is a good offense."* So, Sir with your approval, I will start my offense. If I die, hopefully it will save someone else from dying. But I seem to have many lives and am hard to kill. I will find and eliminate Colonel Oakley's killers, Sir."

"Well Colonel Oakley always said that you had the ability to see the problem and be able to unravel it. So, if I turn you loose on the world, what do I do with the CIE?"

"Make the CIE deputy commander the acting commander, with the normal CIE responsibilities. "

"And if you are killed, what do we do then? "

"That is already a possibility, and if I am in hiding and they didn't come out of their hole and became visible, what would be the benefit. For myself, I think the first thing I need to do while I am here is to talk with the Director of the FBI. Can you arrange that for me Sir?"

"With the orders you have, you can probably go where you want and see whomever you want. But, no one is supposed to see those orders so I will make a couple of phone calls. Give me a few minutes." General Crane then made a phone call. He stated my request and he evidently had his call forwarded to someone else. The General told the person on the other end of the line who I am and repeated my request. He then told the other party, "I appreciate that. I will send General Jorgensen over immediately." He listened for a few seconds and replied, "Yes, Brigadier General Dan Jorgensen is the same man you knew of before as Lieutenant Colonel Jorgensen, Chief of Investigations at the CIE. Very good, he will be right over." He hung up and said, "It is set and you are to go see the FBI Director immediately. Then after you are finished there, return to me ".

Dan was taken by the marine helicopter to the heliport at the FBI headquarters. Upon arrival, he was escorted to the office of the FBI Director, Frank Goodall. While he was being taken to the Director's office, he drew all kinds of stares and once in a while he saw a familiar face. They looked at him with surprise and awe on their faces. Of course, the stars on his shoulders could have some impact on the situation, especially as they knew me as a lieutenant colonel.

Dan met the FBI Director and told him all that he knew and guessed about the situation at Knoxville College, including the loss of around one quarter of a million dollars, the murder of the school's comptroller, and the possible kidnapping of the Osgood children. Dan asked what information had been found about the accountant and auditor at the Knoxville College, Knoxville, Colorado. The Director called for someone to bring the necessary files to him. It turned out that there had been practically nothing done about his former request to investigate those two men, the murder of Mr. Osgood or anything about the Osgood family.

Dan then asked, "Am I going to have some cooperation from the FBI or do I go to the person that issued my orders under which I am functioning?"

The Director puffed up like a bandy rooster and wanted to know who had issued his orders. Dan smiled and then said, "The Commander in Chief of the Department of Defense. Or you might know him as the President of the United States, Dwight David Eisenhower."

The Director was instantly deflated and he sat, in a near state of shock. He calmed himself and then answered, "Of course you will have the full cooperation of the FBI. Your former requests for the investigation of those two men will be done immediately. I assume that you want the financial situations of those two men checked as well."

"Of course. And I want a check made of the Osgood family. In a few days I will be at the Knoxville College, Knoxville, Colorado, and will soon know for myself about the Osgoods. But the sooner they are found and protected the better."

With that, Dan left amid further looks of wonder and amazement from his acquaintances in the FBI. The marine helicopter pilot took him back to the Pentagon... The Marine pilot, it seemed, was enjoying his assignment to ferry Dan where ever he needed to go. Dan then reported to General Crane again and informed him about the meeting at the FBI. The General almost started laughing at Dan's report. "You do know how to stir the pot. Good luck in Colorado. And keep me informed as to how things are going. At least then I will know you are still alive."

Dan saluted, and left the General's office. His next flight in the helicopter was back to Andrews AFB. His plane and pilot were still there and waiting. They took off shortly. This time they had a head wind so the flight took nearly seven hours. The poor pilot and copilot were about dead in their tracks when we landed. I was glad to get my feet on solid ground again. It was now about 2300 hours (11:00 pm) at Peterson Field. I thanked the crew of my plane and left for Fort Carson. This time when I arrived at the main gate I was waved straight through. I guess the word had gotten around as to who I am.

When I got to the visitor quarters, I was again waved in without hesitation. I entered my room only to find not my wife, but a masked man with a gun in his hand. I don't think he recognized what I was equipped with. At the orders of General

Crane, I had been given a bullet proof vest and I was wearing it. I hit the gunman with a right hook that floored him out cold. He had been obviously closer to me as I entered than was safe for him. I snatched up his gun and when another gunman came rushing out of my bedroom, gun in hand and masked, I shot him between the eyes. I then ducked down and to one side. A burst of gun fire came from the bedroom in my direction. Then I heard a 38 special service revolver bark three times and a heavy thud. I went into the bedroom and saw an angry Grace with her pistol in her hand. I then took a curtain cord and tied up the third gunman while he was still out. The one Grace shot didn't need to be tied up, being dead.

There was an urgent pounding on our door with loud verbal requests for our wellbeing. I opened the door and let the security policeman into our quarters. He informed me that backup was on its way. He looked around and said, "I guess they may not be necessary." The backup arrived and shortly the Chief of the Security detachment arrived as well. Colonel Schnell couldn't believe what he saw and apologized up one side and down the other. He then said, "I guess our security is not as good as we figured. General Warner will want answers to this." I then told him, "I will answer to General Warner myself. These people that are after me have tried to get me with ingenious methods. Just check out who these men are and find out how they got in here. Then we'll know more about this whole organization. Let me know as quickly as you can. If I happen to be with General Warner at the time of your report so much the better. I will want to interrogate the live one later"

Grace, Helen and I were then shown into new accommodations. One that was a bit less cluttered. The unconscious man and the two dead men did kind of cluttered up the apartment.

Grace looked at me and said, "Well it looks like things are back to normal again." I looked at Grace with a smile on my face and a glint in my eye and told Grace, "I think an energizing hug and a kiss are appropriate about now". Grace had no problems with this request.

CHAPTER THIRTEEN
Back in the Harness

Three days later, Dan entered the office of the President of Knoxville College, along with four CIE staff, in uniform and armed. His receptionist and secretary looked at Dan, somewhat in horror. She gasped and said, "I don't think President Wilson will want to see you."

I replied, "Well he can see me voluntarily or under a court order, which I have in my pocket. Will you tell the president that Brigadier General Dan Jorgensen, Commander of the Army CIE wishes to see him immediately?"

She arose and walked rather shakily into the president's office. Shortly President Wilson came to the door and reluctantly asked Dan to come in. He looked Dan over and said, "You do know people in high places."

I replied, "On the contrary, people in high places know me or about me. My former commander was murdered in an effort to find me. I was given this promotion and ordered to this position by the President of the United States. You could say that I have some pull at my disposal. I made the Director of the FBI open things up regarding this case. Now I want you to tell me who ordered my suspension. You can tell me or spend time in jail for violation of a court order. This order comes from a source higher than anyone against me can overrule. This I guarantee. Now, will you tell me who ordered my suspension?"

President Wilson looked frightened and stuttered his reply, "My y a wife."

This shocked Dan. "What has she to do with this?" "Her maiden's name is Osgood. The comptroller was her brother. Evidently, she had received a warning and told to make me get rid of you."

"You knew your wife was the sister of Jerold Osgood, your comptroller, and you said nothing when I asked about your comptroller's family! This causes me to have serious doubts about your honesty and innocence in this case. You had better be completely frank with me in the future or you may find yourself in jail for any number of charges ".

"As you can see their orders have backfired on them. I can now call in a number of units of troops if needed. Even four-star generals listen to me and are afraid to refuse any request or order I make. I don't want to resort to such, but I will get to the bottom of this. Now I want to talk to your wife and here in your office, if you will call and ask her to come, if you please. If not, I can have a few men escort her here. Do as you feel best, but I will talk with her." While Dan waited for Mrs. Wilson to arrive, Dan asked. "Were you aware that as I was preparing to leave after you suspended me, I was visited by three members of the Board of Governors?"

"Y yes, they came and talked wi with me. Th hey were n not happy. I am lucky to still be here."

"How long has the accountant been here at the college?" "About three years. He was recommended by our auditor. He had good references." "And how about the auditor?" "He has done the auditing here for four or five years."

Dan thought about this and then asked, "How long had the comptroller been here?" "Over t ten ye years. He has done a gre great job and we ha had no pro problems. U until now th that is."

Dan replied to these bits of information, "Interesting. Very interesting."

Shortly, Mrs. Wilson came in and asked her husband, "What is it dear? Is something wrong? I was visiting with Francine when you called. This better be something serious." Then she saw me and screamed, "YOU!"

I told Mrs. Wilson, "You can calm down and answer my questions or you can spend some time in jail. I will get to the bottom of all of this mess with or without your help. But it will be quicker if you answer my questions. I have authority that no one can overrule. If I had to, I could call in one, two or more companies of infantry, armored units, rangers or paratroopers. But that won't be necessary. They have tried again to kill me and my family. They came up short".

"Now I recommend you sit down. Calm yourself and we can do this quickly and quietly. Otherwise, we will do it the hard way. It is your choice. Who told you to get rid of me? What were you threatened with?"

She looked at me with her eyes as big as saucers and a mixture of anger and fear on her face. Finally, she answered me in a rather quiet voice. "I was told that if I didn't get rid of you, my brother's family would die. It was a man's voice on the phone. I didn't recognize the voice. I have heard nothing about my brother's family since."

"With that bit of information, I will now make myself scarce and hope my presence does not endanger them more than they already are. Thank you. I will call you every couple of days to see if there have been any changes. Goodbye and good luck."

Dan stood and left the college along with his men. Dan's next step was to talk with the sheriff. It had to be done in some way to not let anyone to see me talking with him. Dan called his friend the Lieutenant Governor, John March. When John came on the line, Dan said, "John, this is Dan. Could you call the sheriff here in Knoxville and ask him to come to Denver to meet with you?"

John thought for a minute and said, "I take it you don't want people there to see you meeting with the sheriff." "You got it. When you have a meeting set up, let me know. I will be at Fort Carson. You can call the Post and ask for General Jorgensen." "GENERAL, Dan what has happened? Men just don't get promoted that fast."

"Well, you've heard that it isn't what you know, but who you know. Except in this case. It isn't anyone I knew but who knew of me. When we get together, I can explain more of it to you. Just don't spread the word around too much. I'm one of the targets in a shooting range. Thanks John."

The next day Dan received the call from John March. "Dan, the appointment is set for 1:00 this afternoon. We will meet at the conference room of the Commander of Peterson Field. I arranged that to limit who could see the two of you meeting. I will be there also. I'm curious. Very curious."

At 12:45 Dan was driving onto Peterson Field, he was using his official car, the one with a flag flying from the front bumper with a star on it. They weren't going to stop me, but I stopped anyway. A Senior Airman stepped up to my car and looked in when I lowered my window. He was surprised but recognized me. He smiled and saluted and waved me on through.

I drove to the commander's office building. When I entered a female airman showed me to the conference room and I entered. John was waiting for me as well as the commander of the base. He was a Colonel. He introduced himself, "Colonel Hal Wardell" and said, "we have heard quite a bit about you. You surely have friends in high places." "Friends that knew me, rather than any I knew. Things have happened faster than I can keep up with. Thank you, Colonel, for your hospitality and use of your conference room today. I wish I could invite you to my meeting. In fact, I wish I were not going to take part in this meeting. After some introductions I will require my friend John to wait in another room until I am finished. I don't care for this top-secret gossip or scuttlebutt".

Then the sheriff was ushered in. He recognized the Lieutenant Governor and was introduced to the Base Commander. There was some polite small talk and then I stepped into the sheriff's view. His jaw just about fell to the floor. He then asked, "What is going on here?" The Base commander excused himself and John talked with the sheriff and explained why this meeting was taking place as it was. He then also excused himself and asked Dan if they could have some time after the meeting. Dan agreed with John's request, especially since he wanted that also.

"Sheriff, it is good to see you. There have been some fast changes taking place, not of my request. Colonel Oakley, the CIE Commander was tortured and murdered. All in order to find me. I have been promoted to brigadier general and made CIE commander with my headquarters temporarily at Fort Carson. My orders, from the Commander in Chief, are to find the killers of Colonel Oakley. I am positive that his death is related to the embezzlement, murder and kidnapping that have taken place at Knoxville. I also believe, or I should say, convinced that the embezzlement of the Knoxville College funds was arranged by the accountant and the auditor."

Dan told the sheriff about his questions he put to President Wilson.

"How long has the accountant been here at the college?"

"About three years. He was recommended by their auditor. He had good references."

"And how about the auditor?"

"He has done the auditing there for four or five years."

"The timing is hardly coincidental. I believe the comptroller suspected something and confronted the accountant. The comptroller had been there at least ten years with no problems until the auditor and accountant showed up. And the accountant was recommended to the school by the auditor. Circumstantial, but rather significant. The embezzlement ties in with similar thefts from around the country. I just happened to stick my head into a hornets nest again. By the way, my promotion was ordered by the Commander in Chief. All of this is top secret. I wouldn't tell you if I didn't think I could trust you."

Their meeting ended on good terms and the sheriff seemed a bit overwhelmed. Dan told him, "If this has been overwhelming to you, it is even more so to me. My head is still spinning. I think if we work together, we will come out on top. I am hoping when this is all over, to go back to Knoxville and teach. There is a lot more satisfaction in seeing a student grasp an idea and succeed in life. That is far better than having a knock down and drag out gun fight, even if you win. Destroying life doesn't hold a candle to helping a student find his spot in life."

The sheriff left and Dan then had some time for John. It took Dan about a half an hour to bring John up to date. When he was finished, John whistled. "Wow. So, you were promoted to general, made commander of the CIE and stationed at Fort Carson, all under the signature of Dwight David Eisenhower. That isn't something you hear about every day. Well good luck

Dan. I had better get back to the capital. I suspect the Governor is going to want to meet you. For all this top-secret stuff is hardly secret now, a lot of this is all over the papers. Your whereabouts is not secret any more either. I'll see you later." And John was gone.

Dan went to the Base Commander's office and was shown in. Dan filled him in on as much of what had gone on as possible, his promotion and assignment by the President and stationed at Fort Carson.

He said, "General, I'm glad I'm in the Air Force rather than the Army. I can just see your base commander pulling out his hair trying to accommodate you and your staff and all. Well, I'm glad you are next door. If we have problems, I figure we could use your help. Good luck and welcome at any time."

Dan returned to his visiting quarters to spend some pleasant time with Grace and Helen. They had a carefree evening. The first in days, or was it weeks? They discussed the happenings of the last few days and planned what they would do when this whole thing was cleared up. Dan told her that his wish was to return to Knoxville College and teach. It was a lot more pleasant and satisfying. And more peaceful when they weren't being shot at. She laughed and agreed with him. She liked it there as well. This was all contingent on them being accepted back there. They could cross that bridge when the time came.

With the acting CIE commander at Quantico taking the burden of managing the Element, Dan was more or less free to follow up on finding the killers of Colonel Oakley and Mr. Osgood as well as the kidnappers of Mr. Osgood's family.

Dan got on the phone and called the FBI headquarters. He was able to talk with the Director. He didn't seem pleased with this call from Dan... Dan asked who had been put in charge of the investigations that I had recommended. The Director told him that the Agent in Charge was Richard Owens in Denver. He then gave me his phone number for which I thanked him and closed out the call.

Dan then called the FBI Agent in Charge, Richard Owens. When he answered I identified myself. He was furious. "How did you get my name and phone number? No one can get this."

"I did. In case you don't know who, I am, I am Brigadier General Daniel Jorgensen, Commander of the US Army Criminal Investigation Element, or CIE I have been given rank and command on the order of President Dwight David Eisenhower. I answer to the Army Chief of Staff and to President Eisenhower. I have been given specific orders and you can provide information to me which I need or I can talk with the Director again. He doesn't like to hear from me because he knows what authority I carry. I was instructed by your Director to call you for the information I requested. Now, you can cooperate peacefully or you can cooperate under orders. It doesn't make much difference to me. I can ask you politely or I can demand answers to my inquires. Which will it be?"

"Tell me again what you wish to hear from me."

"I need information on the investigation of the accountant at the Knoxville College in Knoxville, Colorado, Ray Dawson, and the auditor, Leonard Anderson. I would suggest you look into their financial records for a start. I requested this investigation some time ago. This has become critical. I also asked for information on the family of Mr. Osgood, the school's comptroller that was murdered. The comptroller's family has disappeared. Do you have any information on these matters?"

"I don't have any at this time. This hasn't been a priority in my office."

"Well, it just became your highest priority. Or I will go next time to the Attorney General. And since my orders came over the signature of President Eisenhower, I think he will listen to me. Your Director did without hesitation after he found out who I was. Good luck Agent Owens. If you need to talk with me, just call Fort Carson and ask for General Jorgensen. Good day."

Dan was getting rather disgusted with the FBI. They had better get something for me and fast, or else!

Dan then went to the Federal Judge in Denver and described what he needed and why. He also gave him a rundown of his authority and his orders. This whole situation was a

National Security matter. The judge listened to Dan and read the documents Dan provided. At this time Dan was asking for an order to obtain the financial records of the accountant, Ray Dawson, and the auditor, Leonard Anderson for the Knoxville College, Knoxville, Colorado. The judge issued those orders.

Dan then sent one of his operatives to the financial institutions in and around Knoxville. He wasn't long in coming back with an arm load of records. It looked like he had brought back enough information, after a quick review of those records, to order the arrest of those two men and to seize their accounts. These were done promptly. So, Dan has started the ball rolling and he knew he had better wear the bullet proof vest all of the time. And wear his loaded side arm as well.

Dan then visited the Commander of the Security Forces at Fort Carson. He asked the commander how the gunmen were able to enter the visitor quarters and attack Dan and his family. The commander was able to answer it thoroughly as he had investigated that issue immediately after the attack. The identity of the attackers had been determined. They were part of a gang from Denver. They had appropriate IDs that allowed them on the Post. The loop holes were tightened up considerably.

Dan was far more satisfied with the commander's response than he had been with the FBI agents. Dan spent a quiet evening with his family again, for a change. Such evenings were a rarity and much needed to rejuvenate himself as well as Grace. Helen was getting to be rather rambunctious and was a happy little brunet angel with gray eyes and an infectious laugh. Her smile reached from ear to ear and emanated from her beautiful eyes. She was the joyful center of their lives.

The next couple of days were rather dull with little happening and things hopefully developing in other areas at his request or orders. It seemed that he needed to prod Agent Owens again and ask for an update. Dan called him and he was a little more cooperative this time. "We have been able to find nothing about Mr. Osgood's family yet but our men are following up on a few leads. The search of the financial records and contacts of Ray Dawson and Leonard Anderson has led to finding some interesting contacts associated with organized crime. Your arrest of those two seemed to have been none too soon. We are close to being able to indict some big members of the "Family."

"You're doing a good job. I think that together we can close down a big ring that is milking good people of vast amounts of private resources. Thanks for your help. I will see that you get the recognition."

The next couple of days, Dan found himself twiddling his thumbs. Then on a hunch, he went to the finance office on the Post and requested access to procurement record for construction projects. The head of the office, a colonel came out and spoke to him. "I'm sorry sir but those records are confidential and we're not supposed to let anyone see them."

Dan then told him, "I'm not just anyone. I can go to General Warner for approval or I can go to the federal judge and get a court order. The judge is well acquainted with me and rather cooperative. But so is General Warner. Do you wish to let me review those records or do you wish to upset the General?"

"Come right this way. Sergeant House will assist you any way she can."

Sergeant House was an attractive young woman that wasn't pleased to be given this task. She would do what she was ordered but was doing it with prejudice. So be it. She took me to a room with filing cabinets lined along the walls and in enough rows to fill the room. "Sir, do you have any specific projects you wish to look at?"

"Yes. I want one that has most recently been completed and closed out."

She took me to a filing cabinet and unlocked it. There was a table and chair a short distance away where I could sit and go over the files. I then asked for a legal tablet of paper for making notes. This she supplied quickly. I then told her she could go back to what she had been doing.

I began my scanning of the records and making notes of particular entries. I found the pattern I expected, or suspected, rather quickly. I made note of the companies listed with those specific entries, phone numbers and the name of the officer that had ordered or received the supplies requested. Hmm. interesting. I then found a telephone and called Agent Owens.

"Agent Owens, could you send some men to this address", which I then proceeded to give him, "and hold everyone there until I get there myself? If you encounter difficulties, I will have a squad of Rangers there within fifteen minutes by helicopter for backup. I am sure this is a key link in our search. Thank you."

Dan then went to the Security Police commander and requested the Base Deputy Commander and the deputy commander of procurement brought in for questioning. You might want General Warner present for the questioning as an observer and for his information. I will be back in about an hour to do the questioning.

Dan then went to the Ranger Commander and requested a squad of Rangers and four helicopters to take them and myself to this designated location in Denver. The FBI will be at that location and may need fire support or backup.

We loaded everyone into the helicopters and we were off. The Rangers were all loaded for bear. Upon arrival, it looked like the FBI people were in a standoff with gunmen. I called out over a load speaker from my helicopter, "I order you to drop your weapons. We have you covered from the air and we will fire if you do not drop your weapons. I give you three seconds, and I order the Rangers to commence firing if you don't drop your guns ". They dropped them post haste.

We landed and the FBI crew entered the compound where construction supplies were held. The FBI took the gunmen into custody and picked up a small truck load of records. I took the man that looked to be in charge of this bunch of suspected criminals and handcuffed him. I then loaded him into my helicopter and we were off for the return flight to Fort Carson.

Upon arrival I reported to the Ranger Commander and thanked him for the capable assistance his men had provided. I then loaded my prisoner into a vehicle with a couple of Security personnel, armed. We then headed for the Security Police compound. Upon entry, General Warner asked me what this was all about. I told him it would all be clear in a couple of minutes and asked him to come with me. We went to the interrogation room. When we entered, the Deputy Commander and the procurement officer both saw who I had with me and their faces went white as snow. I don't think it was going to require much questioning now. Their faces admitted their guilt.

General Warner recognized their reactions and his face went hard as granite, but he didn't say anything. When the three men were questioned, they each refused to answer and requested an attorney. They were each booked on suspicion of Grand Larceny and accessory to murder. This last charge seemed to throw the Deputy Commander for a loop. I figured that he and the procurement officer after conferring with their attorney would go for a plea bargain to get out of the murder charge.

After the business was completed in the interrogation room, I met with General Warner and gave him a more detailed explanation as to how this event took place. I commended him on the support I received from his security forces and the Rangers. Their help facilitated the operation greatly and I'm sure saved lives. The FBI were having some difficulty subduing the gunmen in Denver until the cavalry arrived to convince them it would be best to surrender.

General Warner said, "I am at a loss as to what to say except that I'm sorry to see this corruption in my own office. I wonder how this could be, even in my own staff and office? I think that I am going to keep a closer watch over my men. Especially those with authority to be corrupted by their own power."

Even so, he was pleased at how quickly Dan had recognized the problem and brought it under control so fast. Dan told General Warner, "I'm sorry to say Sir. But I'm afraid we have just scratched the surface. With this series of arrests, I can expect a number of strong attempts on my life or an attack on my wife and daughter. Even here on Fort Carson."

Then General Warner immediately issued an order to raise the level of security. He wasn't going to allow any attack on his Post if he could have any say in the matter. The change in feeling and tension on the base could be felt like an electrical field.

Everyone acted like cats on a hot tin roof and they were fidgety.

At the gates to Fort Carson, vehicles entering and leaving were searched more frequently and thoroughly to the chagrin of the people having to enter and leave the post. The people knew why and complied, but it quickly tires everyone. At which time complacency begins to set in and the post becomes a prime target. The commanders and supervisors will need to keep close tabs on all of the critical employees, officers and enlisted staff. This quickly discourages almost everyone.

CHAPTER FOURTEEN
Another Head Rolls

I then went to my quarters and was walking up the path with my mind occupied with what had just taken place. As I approached the building, I saw a man wrestling with my wife and dragging her toward a car. I pulled my 45 and ordered him to stop. He dropped my wife and pulled his own gun. I fired and shot him in the leg. That 45-slug put him on the ground.

Then a car screamed out of the parking lot and I fired and hit one of the tires, which is what I wanted. The car careened out of control, hit a tree and came to a stop. The driver got out and held my daughter in his arms. He threatened to break her neck if I didn't drop my gun. I put it on the ground. and he put Helen down and pulled his gun, Grace opened fire. The man never knew what hit him.

About then it seemed that the entire security force showed up in cars with their sirens screaming. They looked the situation over and called for ambulances. About then General Warner showed up, white as a ghost. He was shaken up considerably when he saw the handcuffed wounded man loaded into an ambulance and the dead man removed. The dead man didn't have to be handcuffed, needless to say, but was taken away.

General Warner told Dan, "It looks like you don't need any body guards. You shot and wounded the man with your 45. The wound is obvious. But who killed the other man? And what weapon was used on him?"

I indicated my wife who was hugging Helen. "She is a bit protective of our daughter. She is an expert shot with her 38 special. I'm not sure that I could beat her in a shooting contest. And I wouldn't want to face her in a gunfight. She seems to like the spot between the eyes as a target."

I was grateful for my Colt 45. This pistol was developed for the Army after the Spanish-American War. Occupation troops in the Philippines were being killed by doped up natives with vines wrapped around them and wielding machetes. The natives could be killed with the Army's 38 caliber side arms of the time but they wouldn't stop their attackers and dead or not they were able to hack up our men before the native was actually stopped and was dead. The 45 was designed to drop a man when hit, whether in an arm, leg or where ever. A man knocked to the ground can't attack someone else very well.

The 38 which Grace uses can kill a man but it won't knock them down as readily. General Warner had recognized the wound of the man shot in the leg but not the wounds of the dead man. Dan uses the 45, but the General didn't know who used the other weapon nor the type of weapon it was.

The arrest of two high level officers at Fort Carson seemed to have quieted things down a bit. But it was a bit late to stop the attempted kidnapping which had just taken place. The death of one kidnapper and arrest of a wounded kidnapper put a damper on the situation. But I didn't believe it had stopped. If the theft or embezzlement could go on at Fort Carson, could it be happening at Peterson Field?

I drove over to Peterson Field and asked to see the Commander, Colonel Hal Wardell. I was shown in without delay. I told him of what had taken place at Knoxville College which led me to search for the possible theft of the Department of Defense monies. The search of construction files at Fort Carson led to the evidence of theft and thereafter to the guilty parties. The Deputy Commander and their procurement officer have both been arrested to General Warner's chagrin. I told him how their involvement was discovered and their operation broken up. "Now, I'm curious. If that could be going on at Fort Carson, might it be going on here at Peterson Field. I would like to do a quick review of some of the purchase records involving any construction projects here. With your approval that is. If I find something we can nip it in the bud. If I find nothing, then I would say you run a tight and secure organization. I would prefer the latter. Do I have your permission to do the review I have outlined?"

"Most certainly. If we do have a similar problem to that you found at Fort Carson, I want it found and eliminated as quickly as possible. I will take you to our finance office and introduce your to our staff and instruct them to give you full cooperation. Please keep me informed of any findings, good or bad."

"Of course, and thank you."

We then drove to the finance office and Colonel Wardell introduced me and gave the intended instructions. The staff had heard much of what had taken place at Carson and asked a few pointed questions. I answered them completely. If they truly knew what was going on, they would be far more cooperative. That is if they had nothing to hide. I was given temporary office space and asked for what records I wished to see first off. I told them I wanted to see purchase records for an ongoing construction project on base. These were quickly brought to me.

I began my search. It didn't take long before I found what I was looking for. The same basic organization involved with the theft at Fort Carson was involved here at Peterson Field. But it looked like the guilty person here at Peterson Field was not a high up officer. Not even an Air Force officer. Rather it was a captain in the Special Category Army personnel With Air Force program (SCARWAF) assigned to Peterson Field. Dan gave the orders for the captain to be picked up and taken to Security Police detention. I had copies made of the pertinent records and took them with me to meet and question the captain. As I entered the detention room, the captain looked like he had a boil on his behind. He just about let loose with some choice expletives, or so I figured, and then recognized my rank. And then he noticed my insignia of the branch I was assigned to. His face fell and turned pale.

"Captain, I am Brigadier General Daniel Jorgensen, CIE Commander. I have been going over some purchase orders for the SCARWAF detachment and I find some dubious entries with your signature authorizing the orders. Here, take a look at the copies I have made of these particular entries and explain them to me."

He took a quick look at the entries and said, "I cannot say anything without having an attorney present ". I told him that was fine with me. "I will charge you with grand larceny and accessory to murder. You can plead guilty any time and maybe you will survive in the Army prison at Fort Leavenworth, but I wouldn't bet on that. Or you can tell me who is behind this travesty and get a reduced charge. We could even put you under a witness protection program. No matter how you look at it and decide, you will receive a dishonorable discharge and a record that will hang around your neck for life. What is your choice?"

The captain thought about this for a few minutes, during which I just looked at him and watched him squirm. Then he spoke up. "If I tell you who is behind this, will the murder charge be dropped?"

"Yes."

"Will I be protected?"

"Yes. To the limit that the army can provide. However, that wasn't enough to protect Colonel Oakley, my predecessor. Nor has it provided adequate protection to me and my family. My wife and I have reduced the size of the opposing team by a few ourselves. But we are still alive and healthy. Does that answer your question?"

"I think so. The man that I know of that is the godfather in this area is one of the deputy attorney generals in Denver. His name if Ken Valloy. My name must never be mentioned in this or I am dead for sure."

"Will you make a complete statement about this Ken Valloy and his actions and orders, and sign it? That statement will not be released in court or anywhere else."

"I will make it and sign it."

Dan stepped out of the interrogation room and called for a stenographer to take down the captain's statement. While the captain was giving his statement, I reported to the Wing Commander, Colonel Wardell with Lieutenant Colonel Jameson, the Security Police Commander, present. I explained what I found and ordered the army captain arrested. He is currently making a statement after which he will sign it. If his statement contains adequate information and facts, I will turn the information over to the agent in charge with the FBI in Denver and have a rather high official of the State of Colorado arrested for grand larceny, attempted murder and attempted kidnapping.

I am sure I will have enough information to make these charges stick. And I am sure the leak in the financial system here at Peterson Field has a big plug in the hole. Also, I want to thank you and your people for helping to break up a group that threatened national security. Your command level will be notified of your help and cooperation in this matter."

Colonel Wardell and Colonel Jameson were pleased with the report and thanked General Jorgensen for his actions in their behalf. This case gave them ammunition to request command of their air field and control of all actions on this base. Without that, they are almost helpless.

Dan then went back to the interrogation room area and checked on the captain's statement. It would be finished in about five minutes. It was completed and given to Dan. Dan read the statement. It did have adequate details and specific information to order the attorney's arrest. He went in and talked with the captain. He thanked the captain for his statement and handed it to him for his signature. The captain signed it. Dan then told him, "I will put your protection on the highest level possible. You are definitely more valuable alive than dead. And you would not be very valuable to anyone in prison where you likely wouldn't live out the next month. We will be talking more, soon."

Dan then went to his office on Fort Carson and called Agent Owens. "Mr. Owens, I believe I have some interesting news for you and an exercise. You need to pick up and hold for charges of grand larceny, attempted murder and attempted kidnapping, the deputy attorney general, Ken Valloy. I have enough information to convict him of all charges."

Agent Owens whistled. "Wow, that's a big fish! We will pick him up immediately. I will take a number of federal marshals with me for shock value. This should be interesting. I'll want to know how you dug this up later, but now we need to reel in this fish. Thanks for the info. I will let you know our results immediately."

"One more thing, put someone onto checking his financial records and impound his accounts and assets immediately..."

"Will do."

My next step was to check on Grace and Helen. They were not in our quarters. I asked the security policeman at the door if they went out. He replied that they did not to his knowledge. I instructed him to have the base shut down immediately. I then went to General Warner's office and reported all of what had happened and was now going on. The General looked at Dan and said, "You do like to pick big fights."

The guards at all entrances were questioned to determined if Dan's family could have left or if anything suspicious about any vehicle left the Post. Nothing pertaining to the disappearance of Grace and Helen had been seen or noted.

This could mean that they were still on the Post. The entire 759th battalion of Military Security Police was put on alert and ordered out to search the entire base for Grace and Helen. Nothing was to come in or leave. This included the security force's helicopters without the specific approval of their commander, Colonel Schnell. And only helicopters needed for use in the search and surveillance were allowed in the air. Anyone else trying to lift off were to be shot.

About a half an hour later, Grace and Helen came walking up to the visitor quarters. Dan notified the General and the alert was lifted and the Post opened for normal entry and departures. Dan quickly reported to the General, "My wife and daughter have returned. I have discussed this issue with my wife and the furor her disappearance has caused ".

The General laughed and said, "This was a valuable exercise. We have to do something like this periodically, but this time there was a specific reason and something to look for. Now we won't have to have an actual exercise for another six months. However, with you being here I expect we will be doing actual alerts every once in a while. This will keep my people on their toes."

Following this incident, the guards at the gates were more alert and thorough during checks of incoming visitors and deliveries. The inspection of departing vehicles was also increased. Everyone seemed to hold post security to a higher level of compliance. So, this whole affair had not been a total disaster.

Dan decided to call and report to the Director of the FBI. He called and the Director actually seemed pleased that Dan remembered to call and report. Dan explained what had been the most recent events and their outcomes. He was pleased with the results of the raid in Denver using the Rangers for backup which saved the lives of some of his men. He also liked the results of the arrest of the deputy attorney general of Colorado and that the investigation disclosed the location where the Osgood family was being held and that they were now safe.

These actions had helped the FBI write up some positive reports that would help them with Congress. The Director decided that it paid to cooperate with Dan. Such actions brought results with little pain, effort or expense. This was a good investment of resources with good profitable results for the FBI.

That evening, Dan and Grace discussed the probability of another attack on them and realized the need for their being more alert also. Alert and armed. And Helen was never to be out of sight of Dan or Grace.

In spite of the terrible anxiety of the day for Dan, they were able to relax in peace and enjoy their lives for this evening at least. Even if for only a few hours. They were sure this bubble would burst or blow up at any time and they were just relaxing while they could. Any would be killer or kidnapper didn't realize that neither Dan nor Grace were never without their weapons of self-defense, even if their only weapons were their own hands.

The next few weeks were as calm and free of attack as Dan and Grace had experienced in their married life. The preliminary hearings of the deputy attorney general had finished and he was indicted on all three charges. No further information had surfaced that provided any leads to the killers of Colonel Oakley, but a lead surfaced that lead to the family of Mr. Osgood. The mother and the children were rescued and they were now safe. Word was passed on to Dan that the next time he was in Knoxville, Mrs. Osgood wanted to talk with him. Well, we shall see what that is about.

With things being rather quiet, Dan figured that he could take off for a few days and take Grace and Helen to see her family in Cleaveland. Then on the way back he would stop by

Knoxville and visit the college and see what few friends he still had. Most had indeed been fair weather friends and had turned against him. Dan again remembered his thought. " With friends like that, who needs enemies? ".

Dan told no one that he was leaving, except the General. Then they left later in the day when the end of shift took place. That way they would just be one more car among the many. And they did not drive the car with a generals insignia on it. That was the last thing he needed. The General had arranged for that car to be stored in a secure location out of the way of prying eyes. They got to Cleaveland, or rather to Grace's family home about 7:00 pm to a joyous reunion. Grace's mother doted on Helen, their only grandchild. Dan figured by the time they left she would be spoiled. The next day, Saturday, Dan and Grace went to the lodge to visit Helmut and Gretta. It was a nice, pleasant occasion. Sunday Grace asked Dan to wear his uniform to church again. Dan figured Grace was bragging with Dan being a general now. Well, if that makes Grace happy, so be it.

The church services were very pleasant and Grace saw so many friends. I think many of them were a bit intimidated by me in uniform. This hasn't been the first time. Many questioning stares came my way. When I first showed up at this church, I wore the silver oak leaf of a Lieutenant Colonel. Then the next time I wore the wings or birds of a full Colonel. And now I have a star. I'm sure they thought that was a very fast promotion. Why? Why such a fast promotion? I often thought that myself.

Monday, we left Cleaveland and went to Knoxville. My first stop was the sheriff's office. Unfortunately, he wasn't in. The deputy was rather rude and I wondered what was going on. I left and went to the college. I went to the president's office and had a short talk with him. He was cordial, but on the cold side. I guess my return to this school is no longer an option.

My next stop was to see Mrs. Osgood. I knocked on the door and when she opened it, she almost screamed at me. I asked what is the problem and she hollered at me that her children were gone and it was my fault. I asked if I might use her phone. She reluctantly allowed me to use it. I called Agent Owens and asked what has happened? He would not answer me. So, I left and found a phone booth and called my friend, John March; the

Lieutenant Governor. Dan was unable to talk with John as he was in a meeting. So, Dan and family headed for Colorado Springs.

Dan was in a mild state of depression as he drove toward Colorado Springs and Fort Carson. He wondered what had happened to cause this change in attitude of people against him. But had everyone turned against him? The sheriff was in his office and could still be friendly toward Dan. John was in a meeting and couldn't talk with him. Mrs. Osgood, the deputy in Knoxville, the FBI Agent in Charge and the college president were the individuals that showed antagonism against him. From what Mrs. Osgood had said, he could understand her feelings. But why all of the rest of them? Dan decided that he would call the FBI Director and find out what the problem was. Dan had the leverage to require an explanation.

This is an all too familiar situation. Who is responsible for the change? Whoever is involved, are they the ones responsible for the torture and murder of Colonel Oakley? Where do I look for a clue for this chain of actions? This is going to require some brain work. I need to think this over before I go to sleep tonight. Then perhaps my subconscious can work this over during my sleep.

This is one of the best techniques I have to sort things out. Perhaps tomorrow I hope an idea will come to my mind as to where I need to look.

Dan had a rather restless night. He woke up feeling more tired than when he went to sleep. Well, no brain storm this morning, but I will talk with the General. Perhaps he has heard something about this whole night mare. After a calm breakfast with Grace and Helen, Dan went to General Warner's office. He was shown in quickly. The General had a rather stern expression on his face. The General asked Dan, "So, what hornet's nests have you been stirring up now?"

Dan replied, "To my knowledge I have not stirred up anyone or anything since I left here last week. Can you tell me anything about what has happened?"

, "Your friend, John March; the Lieutenant Governor, called and asked me to pass the word to you that you are not to contact him again. This order came to John from the governor."

"So, I have ruffled some feathers. Whose?" Dan thought about this, I will call General Crane, Chief of Staff.

Dan did call General Crane and asked him the same questions. His reply was, "I haven't heard a thing about what is going on. Tell me what you can."

Dan then explained all that he knew and asked General Crane to call the Director of the FBI and find out from him what has happened.

General Crane did just that. As he listened to the answer from the Director, his face got stern and finally said, "Thanks for the information. I will put my staff onto this. I will call you back in a few minutes."

The General then told Dan that he, Dan, was reported by three different banks to have deposited $100,000 into an account for himself. Dan then asked the General to request from the Director to determine the identity of the teller at each of the banks and check their financial situation and if they had opened new account for themselves and how much money they deposited. General Crane did just that and called back with answers. "The Director didn't want to comply with the request I made but finally agreed. After he has gotten this information, he will call me back. I hope your hunch pays off."

"So do I."

Dan thought about what General Crane had told him, and then asked another question. "Sir, why did the banks report those deposits? That is not the usual procedure. The banks need a court order to do that. Who asked the banks for that information?"
The General agreed with Dan's request for more information and will put the questions to the FBI Director.

The next day, the General called Dan and said, "You hit pay dirt. He told me that the tellers each opened new accounts in other banks and deposited $25,000." He then told Dan the names of the tellers involved, the banks they worked at, and the banks where their deposits were made. He wouldn't give me information about who requested the information about the deposits that has caused this problem. The Director has informed the Agent in Charge, Agent Owens, to cooperate with you "

"That is wonderful news Sir. I will begin immediately to clear this up. And I will get a court order to find out who requested the information about the deposits. Whoever made those requests of the banks had to have inside information."

Dan called Agent Owens. The agent was curt, but cooperative, only because of his orders. Dan asked him to bring a Federal Marshal and meet with me at the first bank in two hours, where one of the tellers worked. The scheduled time came and all three were together. They entered the bank, looked at the name plates of the tellers and told the one they were looking for that she was under arrest. She almost fainted. She was taken to the county jail for holding until they could have the other two as well.

They followed the same procedures at the second bank. This teller did pass out. When she had recovered, she was also escorted to the county jail. When they got to the third bank, they found the wanted teller had left about a half an hour earlier without reason so far as they knew. This was out of character for her. After being given her home address, they went there and stopped her as she was pulling away with her car packed.

The three tellers were taken to Fort Carson and to a detention cell in the Security Police building. Then they began to question the three, one at a time. The three gave basically the same story. They had been bribed to accept the deposits and to swear that General Jorgensen had made the deposits himself. A different person had approached each of the three tellers. The names the bribing individuals used were needless to say fictitious. The tellers did give good descriptions of their bribery agents. The three were booked and were held in protective custody. They were willing to testify when the time came.

So, Dan's name had been cleared up and this was reported to the sheriff in Knoxville, the President of Knoxville College and Dan's friend, the Lieutenant Governor, John March. This report was also given to the FBI Director and to General Crane. This last report was made by the Director. Dan got a call from

General Crane telling Dan, "Congratulations on clearing your name. You are valuable to us. Keep it up. By the way, the FBI checked the cameras in the three banks and obtained photographs of the three bribery suspects. They have identified two of them so far and are in the process of rounding them up as quickly as possible."

All three of the bribery suspects were identified and arrested. They were taken into custody and placed in county jails. This was done by Federal Marshals. It wasn't long before one of the suspects and shortly afterward, a second suspect requested protection They were given that only after they named the person that had hired them to set up the bribes. "Guess who set up the bribes."

Dan didn't have a clue as to who was responsible. "Who was it?"

"Agent Owens. When Federal Marshals went to arrest him, he shot himself before anything could be done and is dead. And he was the one that requested the information from the banks. He already knew the information but did this to have that information known." End of another string, and back to square one. Word was sent to the FBI to put the kidnapping of the Osgood children on top priority.

So, I am cleared and all leads have come to an end. Dan thought about this and came to the same road block. He went to the visitor quarters to be with Grace, and see Helen. At least the end of my day can be pleasant. And it was, for a change.

After supper, Dan and Grace started talking the dilemma over as they had done a number of times before. Dan said after a bit, "I am at my wits end and I just can't see where to go next. I'm lost and don't know what to do."

Grace was startled at his statement. She looked at Dan and said, "Dan, I'm surprised. I have never seen you so confused. But, don't you remember that you have a loose end that needs to be solved and finished. Where are the Osgood children? Who has taken them?"

Dan's eyes almost looked like a light had been turned on

inside of him. He kissed Grace and held her close. "Grace my love. You are my life. I now know what I must do."

The remainder of their evening was spent enjoying each other's company. These times always seemed to rejuvenate each other. Which certainly cleared Dan's mind and sent his brain into overdrive. He was able to chart a path to follow to find the answers to his many questions. Grace was really the spark in his life.

Grace was without doubt the true helpmeet for Dan. This thought brought back to Dan's memory the meaning of the term: Helpmeet. A help in earlier history was a rope or ropes, tied around the wooden ships during times of storms. In order to accomplish this, two sailors would be at the bow of the ship and they would throw a rope over the bow. They then would pull the rope back under the hull. When they were back far enough, they would take the ends of the rope and tie them together. Others would take an oar or pole and put it under the knot of the rope and twist it around and around, tightening the rope. This process would be repeated until they had enough "helps" around the hull. This was to prevent the wooden planks of the ship's hull from springing or popping out. When the hull planks popped out, it allowed water to pour into and fill the hold of the ship, causing it to sink. So, a help is a binding force. And the term "meet" meant appropriate. Thus, the term "Helpmeet" is an appropriate binding force. A good wife is a helpmeet or an appropriate binding force. Wives generally are the binding forces that hold families together.

CHAPTER FIFTEEN
The Fox Hunt is On

On the road again, and I'm driving, or riding, in my official car with a trailing police security car. The trailing car has one security police officer and two CIE officers as occupants. And Major General Warner has sent two Security Police with me, one driving and one as a passenger. Both are armed as well as myself. We are on our way to Knoxville to meet with the sheriff and the president of the college.

They arrived at the sheriff's office and the two military cars, one that was a general's with license plates with one star and a flag with one star on it, has attracted a bit of attention. Dan, along with the three Security Police and the two CIE officers, his guards, entered the building and requested to see the sheriff. The deputy was a bit more cordial than the last time Dan came in. Dan was ushered into the sheriff's office. The sheriff was glad to see Dan. He stood and shook Dan's hand with a big smile on his face. He was also glad to meet the CIE and Security Police officers. They discussed the situation concerning the Osgood children. Dan also explained that the FBI is going to be a bit more cooperative now, since the former agent in charge committed suicide when he saw the Federal Marshals coming for him. Agent Owens was the person that set up me as the bad guy. He killed himself before he could be arrested and questioned.

The sheriff had no new information about the Osgood children except the report that the children had gone to see their aunt but never arrived. Dan asked the sheriff, "Has anyone gone along the route the children would probably have taken and asked everyone along the route if anyone saw the children?"

He said, "No. I didn't think it would yield any useful information ".

Dan told him that it should be done, even if such a long time had passed since their disappearance. Dan also informed the sheriff, "I have sent the word to the FBI Director to put the kidnapping of the Osgood children on top priority. Perhaps the FBI could carry out the task of checking the possible route the children might have taken ". The sheriff was pleased with that and would pass the information to Mrs. Osgood.

Dan and company then went to President Wilson's office. He was polite but not overjoyed to see Dan. He was also surprised about Dan's promotion. He had not been aware of the promotion prior to today since it had not registered with his brain at Dan's last visit that Dan was a brigadier general. Dan informed the president of the latest findings. Pres. Wilson's attitude towards Dan didn't seem to improve any with Dan's latest edition of information. And since Pres. Wilson was no friendlier, Dan didn't feel any great attraction to return to this school after this whole can of worms was straightened out, So Dan and company left and they were heading back to Fort Carson and Peterson Air Force Base. Dan had even stronger feelings against Knoxville College and he doubted that he would return here to teach again.

Their time in Knoxville had not been greatly productive. As much as Dan enjoyed teaching here, he was not sure he would ever come back to teach. There were too many festering sores in this school and town, relative to Dan's presence. Could they heal up and let him enjoy being here again? That will take some time to find out the answers to that question.

Dan called the Denver office of the FBI and found out that the Agent in Charge of this case was Ray McCloud a member of one of the Native American tribes of the Pacific Northwest.. He was pleasant to talk with and was glad to get the information that Dan passed on to him. He seemed anxious to make progress in this case. He evidently wanted to solve this case of the kidnapping of the Osgood children. He and a couple of men would be in Knoxville the next day and start the search suggested by Dan. Dan also suggested that he meet with the sheriff who could give him some information about the route the children would probably have taken.

Dan hoped this action could give them a lead on the children.

Agent McCloud and four other agents arrived in Knoxville the next day. After a short consultation with the sheriff, they went out to canvass the route the children would have taken. About an hour into the investigation, one of the agents was talking with an older woman. The agent asked, "Do you remember the day when the Osgood children turned up missing?"

"Yes, I remember it well and I may have seen the kidnapping."

This was a bolt out of the blue for the agent, but he remained calm and continued. "What did you see?"

"I saw an army vehicle pull up by the children and the two people in the jeep talked with the children. After a couple of minutes, the children climbed onto the army jeep."

"What was the color of the clothes the army people were wearing?"

"The man and the woman both wore blue uniforms. The same color as their jeep, or whatever army vehicle they were in."

The agent asked one final question of the woman, "Why haven't you told an enforcement officer this information before?"

"No one asked."

So, with that information, Agent McCloud concluded that the children were picked up by two Air Force people, or people dressed like Air Force personnel. General Jorgensen would be able to track them down if they were indeed Air Force people.

Dan received the report with the greatest of interest. Now he had something to sink his teeth into. Dan then went to Peterson Field to see the commander of the security forces, Lieutenant Colonel Jameson. Dan asked him, Did two security people, a male and female, leave the base on the day the children disappeared?" The colonel checked their records and showed Dan the entry noted.

"Under whose orders did they leave? "

The colonel checked that and said, "Yours."

Dan told the colonel, "I did not give any orders to the Air Force personnel concerned or to anyone with instructions to go to Knoxville and take the two Osgood children to their aunt. Who were the individuals that went to Knoxville that day? "

Dan was told by Lieutenant Colonel Jameson who the two individuals were that went to Knoxville that day. Dan had the two people brought in for questioning. The two entered the interrogation room. The first, a man, Tech. Sergeant Ellis and the second was Airman First Class Sayers. They were not happy, but there was an element of defiance on their faces until they saw me. They obviously noticed my rank and service insignia and they both blanched for just a moment. Dan instructed that he meet with each of these two separately.

Tech. Sergeant Ellis was shown from the room. Dan then asked Airman First Class Sayers, "Where did you and the sergeant go when you left the base?"

"I'm sorry Sir, but I was ordered to not reveal any information about that exercise."

"And who issued those orders?"

"You did Sir."

"I think you know otherwise, Airman. I now order you to be held for a Court Marshal hearing, charged with kidnapping and an accessory to murder." She suddenly turned pale as a sheet and almost fell.

Dan asked her, "What else did your orders say?"

"I didn't see the orders. The sergeant had them and told me what we were to do. We were to find the girl and boy and take them to their aunt's place where they would be safer."

"Do you remember where they were taken, the address I mean?"

"No, but I could direct you to the place."

"Excellent, we will be on our way in about fifteen minutes."

Dan then instructed Lieutenant Colonel Jameson about how to handle the sergeant. "The airman will go with me, along with a couple of security personnel. I will notify the sheriff and the FBI as to what is going on. Hopefully, we will have the children to safety before the end of this day."

Dan left with the security personnel and the airman in an unmarked car, one without any indication of a government vehicle. They arrived in Knoxville a couple of hours later. Dan contacted the Sheriff and the FBI Agent McCloud and told them that he would be following the airman's leads and one of the security men would pass the information onto the sheriff and FBI. They could begin to cordon off the area where the children might be to prevent anyone from escaping. Dan drove on, following the directions he was given.

Suddenly Airman Sayers saw the house they were looking for and pointed to it. Dan drove on past till they were out of sight of the suspect house. Dan and one of the security men approached the house by foot, leaving Airman Sayers in their car. Dan and the security man stayed behind trees or shrubs to obscure themselves and prevent their presence being seen from the house.

The sheriff's men also arrived and had surrounded the house with the FBI agents being scattered around the house along with the sheriff's men. Dan let Agent McCloud take over and Agent McCloud approached the house. He called out and informed the occupants of the house that they were surrounded and that they were to surrender.

A man in the house called back, "If you or anyone else approaches any closer to this house we will kill one of the children. While Agent McCloud was talking with them in the house, Dan crept closer to the house, crawling on his belly. This was not a pleasant task as he encountered several puncture vines. And they were called puncture vines for a good reason. The puncture thorns of the vines can puncture the skin every bit as well as bike tires. It took several minutes before he was against the wall at the rear of the house. He stood and listened with an ear to the wall. He couldn't hear anyone or anything in the area where he was listening. He worked his way slowly and very quietly along the wall. He came to a window. Listening again, he still didn't hear anything in his area. Dan pulled out a small mirror and began scanning the room, making sure that he didn't reflect sunlight into the room. There was no one that he could see in the room, which was a bedroom. The room was filthy and cluttered.

Dan was able to very carefully lift the window without making a discernible sound, which was lucky. Older homes like this, windows often squeak or squeal when you open them. He quickly and quietly entered the room. Once inside, he looked around and found the children bound and gagged behind the bed, lying on the floor. Dan put his finger to his lips and then untied both of them and removed their gags. He then lowered them out of the window. An FBI man and a deputy sheriff saw this and came forward and took the children away.

Agent McCloud was still negotiating with the men in the house. I opened the door of the bedroom and stepped into the room where three men were watching out the windows. I ordered the men to drop their weapons. They turned on him and Dan began firing. He dropped two of them and the third man shot him. With his bullet proof vest on, he was thrown to the floor by the impact and then he shot the third man. After falling, the man never moved again.

When the shooting stopped, the house was invaded by law enforcement officers from all directions. After entering, some of the men scattered through the house to make sure there was no one else present. There were no others. Agent McCloud looked at Dan and helped him to his feet. The agent asked, "Dan, are you okay?"

"Sure, but my chest hurts like all get out. It isn't fun to be shot even with one of these vests on. I'll bet my chest is going to have one big bruise on it."

Of the three men that had been holding the children, two were dead and the third may survive. They hoped so. That way they could possibly obtain more information and find the big guy at the top. Or maybe the woman at the top. Until they had more information, they just would not know. An ambulance was called for the wounded man and another for the two dead men.

When the scene was all under control, Agent McCloud looked at Dan and said, "You make one hell of a one-man Calvary. You wiped out these three and released the children all by yourself."

"I could not have done it without your distraction."

The children were taken by Dan to the hospital to be checked over to make sure they didn't have any medical problems. The Sheriff had gone to see Mrs. Osgood and bring her to the hospital. After she had seen her children and made sure they were indeed hers and were okay, she searched for Dan. She ran up to him, threw her arms around him and kissed him. She said, "How can I ever thank you? They told me what you did. You saved their lives. I'm sorry I ever accused or doubted you." Dan then talked with the sheriff and Agent McCloud and brought them up to date. Dan thanked Agent McCloud for the work done by his people in finding the information which led to the release of the children. He thanked the sheriff for not abandoning him and providing the back up. They in turn thanked Dan.

Dan moved out to the foyer and was ready to return to his car, along with his driver and passengers when President Wilson came in. He rushed up to Dan with a tentative smile on his face and his hand outstretched. He took Dan's hand and apologized for doubting him. He said, "General, if you ever want to come back here. You can have whatever job you want. Maybe even mine. You deserve it."

"I thank you. But this is something I will have to consider. It disturbs me when it takes no evidence, only veiled accusations and everyone turns against me. Besides, I have never heard of a general being turned out to pasture as an ROTC instructor. I have a ways to go to finish the task I have been ordered to do. Time will tell."

Dan, driver and passengers departed for Peterson Field and Fort Carson. I told the airman that she would not be charged with anything. She would be free and in fact she would probably receive a commendation for her part in saving those two children, helping to eliminate and/or capture three criminals. Such things don't look too bad on one's personal record. She was beaming with this news. Her fellow security policemen would receive commendations as well. They risked their lives to rescue those two children as much as anyone else.

The security personnel were all in good moods when we got back to Peterson Field about 1730 hours, (5:30 pm to the civilian world). I then gave a report to the wing commander, Colonel Wardell and Lieutenant Colonel Jameson, Commander of the Security Police of Peterson Field. I made my report and made recommendations for the commendation for the efforts of the individuals of the security police. Colonel Wardell asked me to write up my commendations and he would take it from there. I just asked to be present when they received their recognition.

The next day I went to Peterson Field and interrogated the Tech. Sergeant. First of all, I instructed him of his rights and the charges that were being filed against him. "You will be charged with kidnapping, grand theft and accessory to murder. With the evidence we now have, you will be lucky to see the light of day as a free man." He just stood there. "If you are found guilty of murder, you could even get the death penalty. Then during the years of appeals, you would face death time and time again. You would come to understand the quote from Shakespeare's Julius Caesar, *A coward dies a thousand times before his death, but the valiant taste of death but once.* You will taste and fear death every day of your miserable life. There is only one way for you to avoid death, tell me who you have answered to in this whole fiasco. Tell me who you get your orders from and you might just live. Think it over while you still have time. If you decide to talk, just ask for Brigadier General Jorgensen".

Dan turned and left without looking back. He left Tech. Sergeant Ellis to think for three days. Then he went to see him again. The sergeant said nothing and Dan turned to leave and the sergeant said, "Wait. I'll tell you. My instructions and money came from the State Attorney General."

"Will you make a formal statement, one with full details, times, what you were to do, how much you were to be paid, and also how you got roped into this nest of rats?"

"Yes."

It took two days for the full statement to be recorded and transcribed. After it was signed, I called Agent McCloud and asked him to get at least four federal marshals and meet me with my crew outside of the State Capital building, in plain vehicles. Have another vehicle available to haul away a prisoner.

"Who are we after this time?"

"I'll tell you when we get there."

An hour later we were all inside of the Capital building and attracting much curiosity. I instructed my crew of Security Police, Air Force and Army, to seal off the entire building for about one half an hour. We then proceeded to the Attorney General's office and entered. We were told that the Attorney General could not see us at this time. I then walked to the Attorney's door. His receptionist tried to stop me but I put her to one side and entered with Agent McCloud and one federal marshal. The Attorney General was with a couple of individuals and I instructed them to go out into the foyer and answer all questions of the FBI agents that were out there. I then informed the Attorney General, "You are under arrest for kidnapping, grand larceny and murder." The Attorney General's face was red with anger and he was furious over this intrusion. As the charges I had explained sunk into his brain, his countenance changed from fury, to disbelief and finally to disbelief mixed with fear. He didn't say anything. I informed him of his rights and turned him over to the senior federal marshal. He was led out with his hands in cuffs. One more large fish captured. The standard procedure of informing a suspect of his or her rights may not have been normal procedure at that time, but it was mine.

About this time John March; the Lieutenant Governor and the Governor himself were there in a grand state of consternation. The Governor almost hollered angrily, "Who are you and what do you think you are doing?"

I turned to John and asked in a calm voice, "John, would you care to introduce me?"

John rather sheepishly introduced Dan. "Governor, this is Brigadier General Daniel Jorgensen, Commander of the US Army Criminal Investigation Element. But Dan, I think you owe us an explanation."

"That I will gladly give you with pleasure. Agent McCloud, will you accompany me?" Dan then instructed the senior Security Policeman to lift the security line and open the building for all traffic in or out. He and Agent McCloud then went with the Governor. Once in the Governor's office, Dan introduced Agent McCloud. Dan then proceeded to explain all of the events that lead up to the arrest of the attorney general. "The attorney general has been charged with kidnapping, grand larceny and murder. We have enough evidence to find him guilty on all accounts plus. He will be lucky to avoid the death penalty sentence. I'm sorry to have put your office into a state of chaos, but I had no alternative. With two members of that office arrested by me for the same charges, you might want to investigate the remaining members for your own safety. If you need more information, John knows how to get hold of me. If that is all, good day gentlemen. Goodbye."

Agent McCloud and I left and proceeded to our separate vehicles. Just before separating the agent said, "You do like big fish."

"Not really, they are sometimes hard to real in. But when I find any guilty person, I will do what I must to land them. And, when I make an arrest, I do so after I'm sure that my evidence will stand up in court. I have a pretty good track record of convictions and I'm sure this one will not hurt my record. But I am not trying to make a reputation for myself. What I have done as a result of my work is to set myself up as a target for would be gunmen and assassins. And this is not a position anyone would seek after nor enjoy. It makes for a life that is not enviable in the least and doesn't make for peaceful nights sleep. And my wife doesn't like it either".

Since the Air Force and Army Security Police had already departed for their respective bases, I was alone for my trip back to Fort Carson. This trip of about 115 miles was a fairly pleasant drive and it gave me an opportunity to unwind before I got to my family. I preferred to do so, so as to leave my work at work and not trouble my family with it. Then just south of Larkspur, which is about forty miles from Fort Carson and in a rather lonely stretch of the highway, my car was hit several times with gun fire. I was not hit. I gunned the engine and took off at a high rate of speed. I got my radio and called for assistance. I was being followed and fired upon. This was getting a bit hairy and uncomfortable. They hit one of my tires and I had to drive off the road with as much control as possible. When I stopped, I began giving return fire. I hit their right front tire and they lost control and crashed. I continued to watch their car but no shots came my way. I continued to watch to make sure someone was not playing possum.

I called on the radio and asked for backup and reported what had happened so far. In a few minutes the sound of sirens could be heard. It sounded like the entire cavalry was coming. Then about the time the state police and sheriff's people arrived four helicopters landed and sealed off the area. About forty rangers and security police from Fort Carson approached me. The senior state policeman also approached me. He seemed a bit confused to have the army enter into this fray. When I got out of my car and he saw my uniform and my rank, he seemed to understand.

The rangers had checked the car that I put out of commission. Then the Ranger Major came to me and said, "Sir what did you need help for: You annihilated your entire opposition in short order. The three men in the car are dead. Two by gun fire it seems and the other died when the car over turned ".

The state policeman asked what had happened. I told him as completely as I could without excess verbiage. He took notes about what could be seen, what I had told him and information about me. He was in awe when I told him, "I am Brigadier General Dan Jorgensen, Commander of the Army Criminal Investigation Element. Shortly before this incident, I arrested the State Attorney General for murder, kidnapping and grand larceny. I have enough evidence that he will be lucky to avoid the death penalty. Until we know the identities of these men that tried to kill me, we won't know if this is in response to me arresting the attorney general or not. I seem to be the favorite target for who knows how many would be killers. This is almost routine for me.

My car would have to be picked up as it would need some repairs before I could drive it again. The major called the base for a tow truck to pick up my car. I took my materials from the car and asked for one of the security police to watch over it until the tow truck arrived and then he could come back to base with it.

The State Police took charge of the vehicle with the bodies of the gunmen in it. They would probably be identified with the help of the FBI. This place was pretty much under control so I got into one of the helicopters and we headed to Fort Carson.

CHAPTER SIXTEEN
Will This Ever End

Dan made necessary reports to the Wing Commander and Security Police Commander at Peterson Field and at Fort Carson to the Commander and Security Police Commander. They were taken back when he told them who had been arrested with sufficient evidence to be convicted of grand larceny, murder and kidnapping. He also explained the gun battle he had on the return from Denver. He thanked the general and security police commander for the assistance rendered for me.

They looked at Dan with a wry smile and asked, "What assistance did you need? You wiped out your opposition effectively all by yourself ".

"Well, it does pay to have a bit of insurance in hard times. Doesn't it?"

Dan then headed for the visitor quarters. How often had Dan reached this state of affairs? He parked his new car, which General Warner provided him, in his parking spot, got out of the car and started for the building. A series of shots rang out and Dan was thrown to the ground by the impact. The security policeman at the entrance to the building saw the person doing the shooting and opened fire himself. The gunman fell to the ground. He would never move again, at least under his own power. He was dead. Dan tried to get up but found it difficult. About then sirens announced the arrival of more security police. Two ran to Dan and looked him over. He had been hit and not all of the hits had been over the bullet proof vest. An ambulance was called for immediately. About then Grace came running from the visitor quarters and was kneeling besides Dan, crying. She had gone through this before and she didn't like this one little bit. It was a horrible, traumatic experience. And Dan didn't care for it himself.

The ambulance arrived and the medical personnel started to examine Dan. He had a couple of serious hits but the ones that could have been fatal had hit his bullet proof vest. He would be okay. Dan was loaded into the ambulance and taken to the hospital. One of the officer's wives told Grace she would stay with Helen, so Grace could be taken to the hospital. This was all too familiar to Grace. How many times were they going to have to go through this. Colonel Schnell took Grace to the hospital.

After Dan had been treated, Grace was allowed in to see him. General Warner came in also. He talked with Dan and Grace. He made a suggestion. "This was the second of two attempts on your life in one day. I think it would be safer for you if you were dead. What I mean is that we could release a news report that you died of the wounds you received tonight. We could see that the truth did not get out till we are ready to turn you loose on the world. We can have the killer identified and turn the CIE and FBI loose as well. Let them ferret out the organization that is after you. Do you agree to let me put this into action?"

Dan and Grace talked this over for a couple of minutes and approved the General's recommendation. The General then called the doctor and other medical staff together and told them, "General Dan Jorgensen has just died ". They didn't quite know what was going on but they obeyed their commander, a commander that they liked and were more than willing to obey and follow. Dan's room was closed off. A security officer was placed down the hall to watch over Dan's room but not call attention to that room.

Dan's wounds were not really serious, not life threatening. Dan was able to walk around the next morning and was healing quite well. In the meantime, the FBI and CIE reported to General Warner on a daily basis. They had been able to identify the killer and they knew what group he was associated with. That group was not known for being killers. The three in the car involved with the earlier attack had not been identified so far.

Now to put forward the plan that Dan had died. That night Dan, dressed as a custodial person, took some bedding to a utility room. He then walked out and got in a van driven by General Warner. He took Dan to an old building where Dan could stay out of sight. There was a bed, food and a restroom. and Dan would disappear. A funeral service would be held for Dan on Fort Carson, with no viewing of a body. The service was attended by Dan's friend, John March, the Lieutenant Governor who gave the eulogy. Agent McCloud of the FBI, and the biggest surprise, General Crane, Army Chief of Staff. The General had a few words to say. His presence and what he said had a profound effect on almost everyone at the service.

Grace and Helen were then moved to Cleaveland to be with her family. Her family members were at a loss as to how they were to handle the situation that had been put in their laps. It was not much less of a loss for Grace. She could not see Dan and she could not tell her family the truth. This did not help Grace one bit and Helen seemed lost since her father was no longer around. She loved her Dad and missed him. So did Grace. It was almost as bad as it would be if Dan were actually dead.

This turn of events had produced quite a turmoil in the Army, especially in the CIE. Colonel Johnson at Quantico was now the CIE commander. Would he be made brigadier general? Time would answer that question.

Dan now wondered, what can I do? I can't show my face. But, if I dress in shabby civilian clothes, rather shabby clothes and let my whiskers grow out, I suspect that I will be almost unrecognizable. So, Dan requested appropriate clothes and the General was able to procure them quickly. Letting his beard to grow out was almost as fast. When he was ready, he arranged for a time he could talk with General Warner without being seen and recognized. If Dan had been recognized, it would blow his cover and the criminals would know that Dan was not dead. The General, when he saw me, was almost bowled over at my appearance. "Dan, is that really you? Who were you ordered to answer to?"

Dan replied, "General Crane, the Army Chief of Staff, the Secretary of Defense or the President of the United States, Sir." General Warner accepted my answer because this had never been mentioned in full, outside of his office.

The General sat, let out a substantial blow of air from his lungs and stared at me. "General Jorgensen, I would not have known who you were had I not been informed beforehand and the confirmation when you answered my question. Now, what do you intend to do?"

"I am not quite sure sir. But now I need a reliable car, but one that is discrepantly looking. One that would fit with my present appearance." Dan was sure the General would have no problem providing such a car. When Dan was ready, he left the base with he and his car inside of a cargo truck so that he and the car would not draw attention when he left. The car was unloaded at an old, unused warehouse. So, Dan was on his way.

Dan went to Knoxville, found an apartment and hung around the bars. They were only a few in number, but they were good places to hear the scuttle butt of the area. Comments about the former ROTC instructor and his death were common topics of conversations with the unsavory crowd. They were not at all complimentary of Dan. The third day of his patronizing such establishments yielded pay dirt. One man that Dan had seen a couple of times was talking rather loudly. He was drunk. The drunk man was bragging about how a man he knew had a lawyer that arranged for that man's death, "That high and mighty officer that would flaunt himself around like he is better than anyone else. He is dead. He won't strut around any more like one of them smart alack fighting cocks."

When the drunk left, Dan paid his bill and walked out. When he got outside, he could not see the drunk anywhere. So, Dan went to the apartment he rented and watched for signs of him being followed. He didn't see any signs but that didn't help Dan to feel any better. Dan changed to other clothes and went to another bar the next day. Dan hadn't been there long when the drunk man came in. However, he was not alone. He was accompanied by three rather burly men. They looked to be dangerous characters. Dan checked on his Colt 45. It was still there. Two of the men strolled towards where Dan was seated. Since Dan had chosen a seat in the very back and in a corner so no one could get behind him. Dan, without being obvious, pulled his 45 and had it ready. The men rushed at Dan and he shot the first man in the leg. He screamed and fell to the floor. The drunk started to run for the door and Dan put a shot in front of his face and ordered him to stop and get down on the floor. He ordered the other two onto the floor as well. Dan then instructed the bar tender to call the sheriff. He didn't waste time in doing so.

It took a couple of minutes before the sheriff and a couple

of deputies arrived. When the sheriff walked in, Dan spoke to him and called him by name and said, "General Jorgensen here." The sheriff was speechless. When he was finally able to speak, he looked at Dan and said, "And how can I take you for Dan?" Dan asked the sheriff to have these four men handcuffed, including the injured man and then call for an ambulance.

Then Dan quietly held a conversation with the sheriff. When he was finished the sheriff had a big smile on his face. He then told the sheriff that the fourth man has critical information and must be kept in solitary confinement at all times, including from the present time. Dan also told the sheriff that he was to be booked as an accessory to murder, kidnapping and grand larceny. Dan suggested the same charges against the three, including the injured man.

The drunk looked about as shocked as one could be and fear came into his eyes, all of which took place after he heard Dan tell the sheriff of the charges that he was to be booked under. He wasn't expecting anything like this. He had figured that they would beat this derelict because it looked to him that Dan was paying too much attention to him the day before in the bar when he was a bit soused.

The four were taken to the jail and booked in. They were all shocked to be charged with accessory to murder, kidnapping and grand larceny. They were scared. The drunk was questioned rather intensely but would answer no questions.

Dan called Agent McCloud. The Agent answered and asked, "How did you get my phone number and who are you?"

"Ray, this is Brigadier General Jorgensen. And before you hang up, you might say that I have been resurrected. Ask me a question that probably only you and I would know the answer to so I might confirm that I am whom I say that I am."

Ray could think of no questions so he said, "What do you have on your mind?"

"I have a suspect under lock and key in Knoxville that can possibly identify the person that ordered my death. I figure that the best place to hold him and his three compatriots would be in detention facilities at Fort Carson. Do you agree or do you want to take charge of them?"

"Well, I think I'll let you keep charge of them. But I will want to come and question them if I might."
"Be my guest."

I then called General Warner and asked for four vehicles to transport some suspects to the holding facilities at Fort Carson. "Sir, I will fill you in as soon as I am back on base and cleaned up. I want to take a detour through Cleaveland on the way back."

"By all means general. I'm sure your wife will be glad to see you. I'll be glad to see this walking dead man." And he laughed.

Dan went to his rented apartment and shaved and put on his uniform. He then went and checked out. The landlady was totally flabbergasted when she found out who this renter actually was. Then she was thrilled. She had a famous man renting from her and stayed in one of her rooms. She could call it the General Jorgensen Room and maybe get more rent for it.

When Dan rolled up at the Herndon home and got out, you could hear the screams and hollering all the way down the road. Grace was out and into his arms faster than greased lightning. Helen was there too, as fast as her little legs could carry her. It was indeed a joyful reunion. And since it was Saturday, Dan was asked to stay over and go to church the next day. In his uniform of course.

Monday, they drove back to Fort Carson. Since the word had not been given out that General Jorgensen was not dead, there was a bit of confusion at the main gate. That was quickly cleared up and Dan was given a hearty welcome home by the security people at the gate. One officer smiled and said, "I guess this can explain the four unknown prisoners we have in our detention."

Dan assured him, "Yes, they are there because of me. I hope we can make use of them and that they will become a bit more loquacious. If they talk, I'm sure we can learn some important information. Well Lieutenant, I guess I had better go and report to the "Old Man". And then I have to report to General Crane." The lieutenant suddenly had a queer expression on his face when Dan mentioned General Crane. Dan figured he would know the meaning of this shortly. As he was driving onto the base, he noticed that the flag was flying at half-mast. This caused a ripple of dread go through him. Did this mean that General Crane was dead? I hope not, he is, or was, a good officer and man.

Dan arrived at the command post and entered. You'd have thought they saw a ghost when Dan walked in. Dan decided that thy had not been told he was still alive. It caused a bit of a stir upon his arrival and at first, they seemed to be in shock. When the shock wore off there was a shout or cheer

General Warner came out to see what the ruckus was all about. He looked things over and then said, "I guess I should have warned my people that you were alive Dan."

"Yes", I said and smiled. "It is good to be back Sir. But the reaction the lieutenant gave at the main gate was strange when I told him I would have to call General Crane, and then I saw the flag at half-mast. Does it means General Crane is dead, Sir?"

General Warner frowned, ducked his head momentarily and then nodded his head. With that we went into his office and he closed his door. The general told Dan "General Crane's plane hit some geese on approach to Andrews AFB and crashed. All on board were killed. I have been picked to be the deputy for the new Chief of Staff. While this whole thing was a big surprise and a bit of a shock to me, it is something I could not turn down ".

"Congratulations Sir, I suspect this means a new star on your uniform."

"Yes, it does. I am sorry to be leaving here, but one doesn't turn down a promotion. When you do, you're through in the military. Will you keep me informed as this thing plays out?"

"Yes Sir, I will be glad to and I'm proud for the time I have been able to work with you. You are an excellent commander. One who is concerned with and about his people."

"Thank you, Dan., I try to do just that. When you do that, you have the trust and confidence of your men and women."

The change of command took place one week later. The new commander was Major General Vickers. And I hoped that he was similar to or as good as General Warner.

On the day of the change of command, the new General was introduced to Dan by General Warner. General Warner told General Vickers that Dan had been a major assistance to the base and a good man to have around.

General Vickers looked at me, smiled and said he was glad to meet me. He had heard a bit about me and said, "Evidently, from what I hear, you like to stir up trouble".

I answered that remark, "No Sir, I don't like to stir up trouble, but it seems to seek me out. There are a number of big shots that are afraid of me. I tend to put the guilty behind bars. So, I don't have to find them, I let them come at me. I take their shots at me and then I let them have it. I'm the one that has survived so far."

"Well so long as I'm not one of your targets."

"Should you be Sir?" I turned and walked away.

I heard later that General Warner warned General Vickers, "General do not ruffle Dan's feathers. Those that do wind up dead or in jail. Dan is a good man. Especially if you are on his side."

I had the feeling that General Vickers and I were not going to be on the best of terms. I wonder if General Warner told General Vickers about my promotion and orders. That I was to report only to the Army Chief of Staff, the Secretary of Defense or to the President. I don't think General Vickers would like that. I would in the future report to him only when I had information that was directly pertinent to this base. Otherwise, I would follow my chain of command. I don't think General Vickers realizes just what authority the CIE has in the Army. I hope he doesn't have to find out the hard way.

The next two or three weeks were rather quiet. I spent some time questioning my prisoners that were in detention. The man that had been drunk and hired the other three to beat me up was not cooperative at all. A couple of the other three were a bit more cooperative and gave me some information. They wanted to know when I was ready to have a hearing to determine charges against them. I told them I would hold a hearing when I knew just which charges, they were actually guilty of and what information they gave me. The other two, the man I shot and the drunk were about as closed mouthed as they come.

The two more cooperative men soon started talking. The information I got from them wasn't enough to really do anything against the other two, but I am patient when patience is necessary. I could wait.

On one occasion of questioning the drunk man, I told him, "After I am able to check out the information from the other two to put another nail in your coffin, I will charge you with accessory to murder, attempted murder, kidnapping, and grand larceny. I will have enough evidence to put you away for three lifetimes or death by firing squad. I understand men are getting in line to be on your firing squad. You better hope that they are good shots or that they don't miss intentionally and just severely wound you ".

My talking didn't seem to be making a dent in his shell. I needed to find out more about this man. I felt sure that the answer to this mess was still in Knoxville.

The next day I left for Knoxville with my usual entourage. One Security Police officer was driving and two more were in the car behind us. The drive to Knoxville had been pleasant and uneventful. Our first stop was the sheriff's office.

I went in and got in to see him immediately. I asked him for all information he had on the man that knew who had me shot. He pulled out a folder. It was thick. He showed me a desk in his office and told me I could sit there and read the records. He even gave me a writing pad so I could write down any information I thought may be useful. I spent two hours going over the file and taking notes.

Then I asked for information on the man I shot. His folder was not quite as thick. I was able to extract the useful information in thirty minutes. I thanked the sheriff. Then I and my crew departed.

One piece of information in the files showed the addresses of both men being the same. We drove there and found a rather run-down boarding house. I and one Security policeman went in and found the manager. I asked a few questions but got no information of value. I asked if I could see their room. She said, "Not without a warrant." I told the security policeman, "Stay here and watch every move this woman makes." Then I told the manager, "I will be back in about one-half hour with the warrant. And, if you were to go to the room of these two men, I will see that you spend some time in a nice Federal Prison. And I can do that.?

I was successful at obtaining a search warrant rather quickly and went back to the boarding house. The officer told me, "She didn't even stir from the room. She received no phone calls, nor made one, had no visitors and no one came or went from this run-down rat hole." The manager looked displeased with the description of her building. I showed her the warrant and then she showed me the registration book and found the room where the two men lived. She then took us to the room and let us in. We made a rather quick but thorough search of the room and found nothing of help. She asked if we needed to look at the storage room where many boarders kept their luggage and other stored items? I was surprised at this but refrained from showing a reaction to this information. I jumped at the possibility of seeing any possible possessions of the two men. She took us there and showed the stored items of the two men. We started through them with what looked like a tedious boring job and I didn't expect to find anything. But there was only one way to be sure. We continued the search.

We were nearly through when the security officer whistled and his eyes gaped. He was holding a small note book. He showed it to me and I was astounded. The book contained payments from a prominent Congressman VanDemyer and notes on the job the payments were for. The last one for the killing of me. I took the book for evidence and told the landlady if she said anything about me confiscating this book for evidence,

I would see her imprisoned for aiding and abetting a criminal. I am pretty sure I would and could. And if she thought that, she was correct.

The congressman is the representative for this area. Interesting. What other contacts does the congressman have? I'm sure the FBI Director would love to see this information. With what we had, I figured we had best be getting back to Fort Carson for security. We headed back as fast as the law would allow. We made a call by radio for an escort from where ever we met back to the base. The escort was on its way. We figured to meet the escort in about one hour. I had all of the security men to have their guns at hand and ready. What we were carrying could cost a person his life. I hope that wasn't going to cost any of us this price.

CHAPTER SEVENTEEN
Surprise Move

We were making good time when two state police cars pulled alongside and ordered us to the side of the road. I signaled no. They tried to stop and began to fire on us. I pulled out my 45 and returned the fire. I hit the tire of the lead police car, causing it to swerve and the second car had to stop rather than hitting it. When the single police car caught up with us our escort of two armored cars and six sedans with sixteen security police and rangers as occupants of those vehicles had arrived. The State Police backed off. We stopped and I walked over to the State police car. I left the record book in my car.

A State police officer got out of their car and approached me. He was surprised at my rank and then almost shocked when he saw the CIE on my collar. He said, "There was a report of impostor army people that had taken some important documents from a residence in Knoxville and were heading north. We were trying to stop and arrest you. When we saw the strength of your army force, we began to question those orders."

I told the state officer, "Contact two men. FBI agent Ray McCloud and John March, Lieutenant Governor. They would vouch for me, Brigadier General Daniel Jorgensen of the US Army Criminal Investigation Element. If that isn't enough support, you can call the Army Chief of Staff, The Secretary of Defense or the Commander in Chief of the military, President Dwight David Eisenhower. These are the men I answer to."

He began to apologize and I complimented him and his fellow officers for trying to protect the people and promptly pursuing possible criminals. I then told him, "We have in our possession some critical information that was going to put some dangerous people behind bars." I also instructed him, "Have the landlady of the apartment building, where we had conducted the search under a warrant, arrested and held for questioning for attempted hindrance of a criminal investigation." With that we left and headed for Fort Carson ASAP.

We made quite a spectacle as we entered the base. General Vickers was there red as a beet and ordered me off the base. I told him, "You will have to go over my orders, which no one can go higher than the source of my orders, to order me off this base. And if you don't pull in your horns, I will have you reduced to a major, pulling grass out of the parking areas. And don't think I can't do that. My orders are issued by our Commander in Chief, Dwight David Eisenhower. You just better hope I don't write up a report on you and send it to the Chief of Staff or even the Secretary of Defense. They know me and will listen to me when I report that you are hindering an investigation of a national security situation, that is of top priority. Now General, do I make myself clear. You do not interfere with CIE operations or you are toast ".

Since the General had started bawling me out in public, I let him have it with both barrels. All in front of who knows how many of his men and women watching in awe. I had the impression that there were a number with grins on their faces. And with the General's action towards me, I suspect he had burned a few individuals on the base already. His success on this base was now toast. He had brought this on himself.

I wonder who the next commander would be. I won't have to write anything up but this will get to the top. I'm sure Lieutenant General Warner will be surprised and tickled when he hears about this. I'm also sure the new Chief of Staff will probably want this man's head. But we will see. If this man straightens up, he could become a good commander. Maybe he needs this chance.

Two days later, General Vickers came to my office. He asked if he might come in and I told him. "Sure, this is your base ".

He entered and closed the door. He then apologized for his actions. He said, "I let my emotions control my head ".

I agreed with that evaluation and told him, "If you want the trust and confidence of your people, treat them with respect and you will get it in return. I am here under the orders of the President and I have a job to do. I am not here to run rough shod over you or your people. Your people and I have gotten along fine. I have been able to provide some critical support and I in turn have been provided with great support, to the benefit of this

Fort, this State and this nation. My orders have not been completed. I hope they will soon be done. Then I can let this Fort get back to a more normal operation. But I will do what the President ordered me to do ".

"I'm sorry that I turned loose on you, but you started on me in public so I felt it necessary to set things straight in public. General, you have a great chance to be a good commander. But what you did at the gate is not the way to do it. Ease back a bit. Learn your people and their capabilities. Trust them and they will meet that trust whole heartedly. Good luck General ".

He bowed his head, thanked me and left the room. I took my evidence to the federal judge and presented it to him. He looked it over with a severe frown developing on his face. When he finished, he whistled. "I've heard you like big fish, but this one is very big. I will turn this over to the US Attorney General. I think he will like this job." I left and returned to Fort Carson.

I then went to see the man that tried to have me beaten. He was just as hard shelled as he had been all the time since he had been arrested. Dan asked him, "Well are you ready to talk?"

The man just laughed. Dan pulled a paper from his pocket and began to read it, line after line. The man stopped laughing. He was looking at Dan with his mouth open and his eyes as large as saucers. "Where did you get that?"

Dan just said, "With this information I don't need your testimony. This will allow us to prosecute your boss. So, we can just turn you loose. I will have you released later today."

"You can't just let me go. I will need protection. Without that, I will be dead within one or two days."

"Why will you be dead?"

"With the information you have they will think I squealed and they will kill me."

"Who will kill you?"

"I I ca can't tel l you ".

"Then I can't help you. Had you answered my questions I could have protected you. But you were a smart alack and played hard ball. I cannot help you. Good luck on the outside,"

"Wait, I'll tell you everything. Will you protect me then?"

"I will have a stenographer come in with a tape recorder. Your full statement will be transcribed and typed to make a written statement for you to sign. Then if the information checks out, you will be put in the witness protection program. If you need one day, two days or whatever, I want everything you can tell us. So, as soon as the stenographer is ready you can start talking".

Dan arranged for the stenographer and a guard to protect her during this man's confession and statement. It was on the third day when the typed copy of the statement was given to Dan. He read it over. Then he sat back, wiped his forehead and whistled.

Dan called Agent McCloud and briefly told him of the contents of the statement and asked for a small army of agents, U.S. marshals, state and local law enforcement officers to round up all that were named in the statement. Dan told Ray McCloud that he would arrange for a number of Rangers and security police to help carry out the required net to catch this horde of killers and thieves.

This would be one of the biggest busts ever made. This went way beyond the borders of Colorado and it included some so-called big fish.

Dan went to see General Vickers. I would need the help of a company of Rangers and an equal number of security police to round up the criminals named. Named with enough information to put the lot of them behind bars and some to receive the death penalty.

General Vickers eyed Dan for a minute and then said, or asked, "You are serious aren't you? And you need this many men to carry this out? Why?"

"There are just over thirty individuals here in Colorado,

another twenty-five in Wyoming, Ten or fifteen in Utah, an equal number in New Mexico and a few more in Nevada, Arizona, Kansas and other surrounding states. A total of over one hundred and thirty-five individuals. Some of which are prominent citizens in high places. This will make every newspaper in the country and the help you provide will be mentioned to the benefit of this fort, the army and you. This won't hurt your standing and it will be a good training exercise. Do I have your approval for the help required?"

"Of course. Just let me know as soon as possible when this is to take place."

"Yes Sir. And Sir, no word of this operation is to go beyond this room until the necessary information is needed for the planning of it. When this operation, is over, I will write up a complete report for the Chief of Staff and other levels of command. An article in the *Stars and Stripes* wouldn't be a bad idea either."

Dan then took a copy of the statement and went to Denver to meet with Agent McCloud. The agent read the statement and looked pretty much like he had been hit with a baseball bat. He sat there for a couple of minutes and then said, "Do you realize how much coordination this is going to take?"

The coordination for the entire net to round up the criminals took ten days and we were ready to go. I then made the final arrangements with the security police and Rangers and they were ready also. The next day the trap was sprung.

It happened that the prime individual to arrest was Congressman VanDemyer of this area, and he was in Denver at this time. I went with the crew that were to pick up the congressman. Our crew included myself, Agent McCloud, the senior US Marshal and one security policeman, a captain, and a Ranger with the rank of Major. Five men in all. When we walked into the congressman's office, his assistant wouldn't let us in. I asked him, "Do you want to be arrested for defying a court order?"

He finally stepped aside and let us in. The congressman was furious when we interrupted him. I informed him of his rights and said, "I am Brigadier General Daniel Jorgensen of the US Army Criminal Investigation Element. And I arrest you for murder, grand larceny and kidnapping. You will have your day in court. I then handcuffed him and we led him out of the building.

The rest of the roundup took place with efficiency. In all, one hundred and twenty-three individuals were picked up. Some were turned over to the state prosecutors of the states in which they lived and committed their crimes. Select individuals were turned over to Federal agents and some were turned over to the US Attorney General. The congressman was included in that group.

The trials lasted about three months. During that time I spent more time in courts all over the country than I had time with my own family. The successful prosecution rate was about 97%, or one hundred and nineteen were found guilty of the charges against them. The congressman was also found guilty and was given life in prison five times over in succession. He would never be free again.

The news articles about this whole affair hit every major newspaper in the country and most of the major papers in other countries. The reports made to Army chains of command resulted in big headlines in the *Stars and Stripes*. The attention General Vickers received built up his standing in the army. He even began to treat his people with respect and got it from them in return. It looked like he would be a good commander after all.

The after effect of the investigations, the roundup with the months of traveling from state to state and around the nation was about as hard to take as the stress during that time. And when it was all over, it was as if there were nothing. It created a sense of emptiness. Grace and Helen filled most of the void with pleasure. But when you have been tied up so completely and now that was all gone, it is not easy to make the transition. How do you fill the resulting gap. I hope I can become engrossed with my family, my life, or more like in our lives. At least they should be my life. I feel guilty for not being able to devote my entire being to my family. I hope to be able to return to my life with my family.

I still haven't tracked down the killers of Colonel Oakley! When I get my life sorted out and put again into proper priority, then I can use some clear minded time to this obligation.

The aftermath of the hectic efforts of the past months has left us a bit free. Free to enjoy one another. I have taken some time off and we went to Cleaveland to visit Grace's family. I guess by now I should say our family, since I have no family that accepts me. Grace's family seem to accept me and I enjoy being around them, so, they are my family.

The boys hang onto all my words and are fascinated with my work. They are impressed by the military. I hope to teach them that other fields of study can be just as exciting and beneficial.

Grace is having fun and enjoying her family. She especially enjoys talking and working at the side of her mother. Grace's father and I are having some interesting conversations. It is good to have discussions about other topics than the military and law enforcement. The discussions I have with him are more uplifting and leaves me at peace. At peace with myself, my family and with everything around me.

Every once in a while, I think about the task of finding Colonel Oakley's killers. I don't have much to go on but I know I will have to go to Quantico. Maybe there I can begin to pick up a trail. Quantico doesn't bring back pleasant memories for myself nor for Grace. And since Helen wasn't born during that horrendous time, she will find it new and hopefully interesting.

While in Cleaveland, I visited frequently with the Schmidts... It was a pleasant time here in Cleaveland, and peaceful. I could get used to this. We had great conversations whenever I was able to spend some time with my friends. Helmut and Gretta were grateful to Dan for their new lives since coming to America.

After spending a week in Cleaveland, Dan had to return to Fort Carson. He would go by way of Knoxville and visit a couple of people. His first stop was to see the Sheriff. The Sheriff was especially interested in the outcome of the big roundup. Dan told him the details that were not in the newspapers and the

Sheriff was pleased with the results. He told me that Mrs. Osgood and her sister both wanted to see me. If it is okay with you, I can make a call and they will come here. Is that okay with you? I nodded my head. He made a phone call and then we returned to our talking. In about ten minutes the two women came in with the two children. The children ran to me and hugged me and thanked me. Mrs. Osgood came to me, put her arms around me and kissed me. It seemed like she couldn't speak. Her sister said it all for her. She quietly apologized for blaming me for the kidnapping of the children We made some small talk and then they excused themselves and said goodbye and thank you again.

Then the sheriff told me that President Wilson wanted to see me and wanted me to stop by. "And, he asked if you could wear your uniform when you came by?"

"I suppose I could do that, but I'm not really inclined to even visit him. But I guess I can swallow my pride and comply with his wishes. You might tell him I will be there in about an hour, that is if I can use your rest room for a few minutes?"

"Go right ahead. I will call him now."
I changed into my uniform, fruit salad and all.

Our next stop was at Knoxville College. The campus seemed almost deserted. But this could depend on class schedules. I and my family approached the administration building where the president's office was. When I walked in., the receptionist just nodded to me with a grim expression on her face.

When I knocked on the door of President Wilson's office, he said "Come in ". I walked in and there was a loud cheering. All of the ROTC students and several others from the other classes were there. The ROTC students saluted and were beaming at me. They seemed to be staring at the stars on my shoulders and snickered. I told them of my promotion under the orders of President Dwight David Eisenhower. They cheered again. President Wilson came forward and expressed surprise at how my promotion came about.

President Wilson then asked me again, "General, will you come back and teach here. You touched the lives of your students like no other teacher I have ever had the pleasure of witnessing. You are a natural and tremendous teacher." The students clapped loudly again and held their breaths of expectation.

Dan told them that I would consider that. But first of all, I still had an order from the President to complete. I must find the killers of Colonel Oakley. When that is done, I will give you my answer."

There was a round of hand shaking and the students looked at me with pleading in their eyes. It is difficult to say no to their visible desire for me to return.

We returned to Fort Carson. I went to General Vickers' office and asked to see him. I was ushered in almost immediately. "Sir, I have one last order issued by President Eisenhower. That task is to find the killers of Colonel Oakley. That occurred at Quantico. I find it difficult to do a credible investigation for an event that took place 2000 miles from here. I must return to Quantico. As soon as I can make the necessary arrangements, I will leave Fort Carson and return to Quantico. I appreciate your cooperation and help Sir."

General Vickers stood and came around his desk and shook my hand. "I am genuinely sorry to see you leave, but I understand. Good luck Dan."

Dan then called Colonel Johnson and informed him, "I am returning to Quantico. I am not coming back to Quantico to take over the CIE, rather I am coming to be able to investigate the murder of Colonel Oakley. I will call the Chief of Staff and tell him of my decision and make sure it meets with his approval and to leave you as commander of the CIE". Colonel Johnson took my declaration calmly, but I'm sure that he hoped that he would be able to remain as commander. He would if I had anything to say about that. He said he would have a house available for us when we got there.

Then I called General Warner, Deputy Chief of Staff, and told him of my plan to investigate Colonel Oakley's murderer and asked for his opinion. He agreed with me and said he was sure the Chief of Staff would agree also. Then he transferred my call to him.

The Chief of Staff listened to my decision and then approved of my move. He would consider my recommendation to leave Colonel Johnson as commander of the CIE. "By the way, when you get here, President Eisenhower would like to meet you."

My next step was to meet with the Wing Commander and the Commander of the Security Police of Peterson Field. They had been such great supports during my stay at Fort Carson.

A moving van was arranged for to move our household goods to Quantico. It is a bit funny, we had not been in our living quarters at Fort Carson long enough to get used to them. My car with general's plates on it would also be shipped to Quantico.

We took our time driving to Virginia. We stopped frequently to see sights and to have fun with Helen. We enjoyed nearly all of the trip, but it was long. We finally arrived at Quantico. As we came to the entrance, the guard stopped us and stepped to our car and asked our destination. I told him CIE headquarters. He asked for identification, which I immediately showed him my Army ID. He took a quick look at it, stepped back and saluted and waved us on. They apparently knew we were coming. We drove to the CIE offices and we got out and entered the building. Even though I was in civilian clothes, when I entered, everyone jumped to attention. Colonel Johnson came out of his office and welcomed me and my family to Quantico. He then invited us into his office.

He informed me that he had received orders naming him CIE commander with a promotion to brigadier general. They were waiting for me to carry out the promotion ceremony. He thanked me for recommending him as commander of the CIE. I told him that this was a better solution than making me CIE Commander. This left me free to carry out my assignment. He looked a bit funny when I said that and pulled some papers out of his desk. They were my orders.

I read them and experienced one of the greatest shocks of my life. My orders put me in the pentagon on the staff of the Chief of Staff to work with General Warner. It also gave me a second star. I am now a Major General with the Promotion ceremony taking place in three days, along with the promotion of Colonel Johnson.

CHAPTER EIGHTEEN
"Vengeance is Mine"

Somehow, this didn't relieve me of my original task and it didn't seem to ease the warning that I detected. I am sure that there will be more attacks on my life. Well, one thing at a time.

I was given a home on Quantico. Maybe I'll have the chance to show Grace around this base yet. We were shown to our home and found our belongings had been moved in and unpacked. My car with one star on the plates now had plates with two stars.

The next day I went to the Pentagon to report to the Chief of Staff. I asked for an escort since I knew very little about the arrangements of that complicated structure. I reached the offices of the Chief of Staff and entered, thanking my escort. When I entered, General Warner was there to welcome me. He had a big grin on his face and a twinkle in his eyes. His welcome was enthusiastic and genuine. He asked, "Why aren't you wearing your second star?" I told him that the promotion ceremony would be in two days.

General Warner then took me to the Chief of Staff's office and introduced me to General Bruce Austin, the four stars showing rather prominently. General Austin seemed like a likable man. He welcomed me to his staff and looked at me as if he could see right through me. I wondered what he could see. General Austin then made a quick phone call. I couldn't really hear what he had to say, but I thought he was making arrangements to have me meet someone. After he hung up he said, "Dan, do you mind if I call you Dan?"

"I don't mind at all sir."

"Then, in that case, I would like you and Lewis to come with me."

We went down to the parking level of the Pentagon and got in General Austin's car, one with a cluster of four stars on the plates. We drove out from the parking garage and headed into the District of Columbia. We arrived at the White House where the guard waved us on in. I was sure by now who I was going to see. We were escorted to the President's office, and entered. His secretary stepped into the Oval Office and told the President that we were here. She then indicated for us to enter. General Austin stepped into the oval office and saluted. General Warner and I also saluted when we entered the room. President Eisenhower was a very dignified man.

He had already met General Warner and met with General Austin frequently but had not met me, even though he is the one that issued my orders personally. He walked around his desk and came straight to me and shook my hand. He had a pleasant smile on his face as he said, "General Jorgensen, it is a pleasure to finally meet you. I have heard great things about you."

"The pleasure is mine in meeting you, Sir."

"Dan, after you've had a chance to settle in, I would like you to come so we can have a good talk. There are some things I would like to hear about. One thing is that you have had quite a run at finding and prosecuting high ranking criminals. You do ruffle feathers and catch the fallout. I hope the opposition will never be able to eliminate you. We need you. Good luck and come back quickly."

With that polite dismissal, we left and went back to the Pentagon. Back in the Army Chief of Staff's suite of offices, General Warner showed me my office. My impression was that a person could get lost in there. After a short time I was called into General Austin's office along with General Warner. Then General Austin began to tell me of my responsibilities. After he was finished, he asked if I had any questions. I did.

My first question pertained to finding the killers of Colonel Oakley. "Do I still have the task that had been given to me by President Eisenhower to find the killers of Colonel Oakley?"

"That is a difficult question to answer. This task has not been discussed. Perhaps you may ask that question during your meeting with the President in the near future."

"So, what is my primary job here in the Pentagon?"

"Stay out of gunshot range. You are too valuable of a man to let some gunslinger prove he has guts by shooting you. You have put more people, including more high-ranking officials in jail in the last year than the entire FBI, CIE and most state enforcement people put together, and those people you put away needed to have that done. But you have some dangerous people scared enough to declare a world war with just you on the one side and everyone else on the other. We need you here where we can hopefully keep you safe and be able to use your brains to put them out of business."

"Those are two massive jobs. One for me putting them out of business while I sit behind a desk and one for you, the army, security police, CIA, NSA, FBI and everyone else you can think of to watch my backside. I was nearly killed on Quantico and again at Fort Carson, about the two most secure installations in the US. How do you think you will keep me safe when my family is totally vulnerable? The best defense is the best offense. If I can scare whoever is behind all of this, the better chance we will have of eliminating them. Turn me loose. That is your best chance. If they focus on me then they may ignore Grace and Helen."

"Well, you may be right, but I will have to run this by the Commander in Chief. We will see what comes up. But in the meantime, keep your head down ".

The home assigned to me and my family on Quantico is the same one that we had for a day or two back when I was shot on Quantico. That one came close to doing me in.

The next day was the promotion Ceremony for me, receiving my second star and for Colonel Johnson to receive his first star. Lieutenant General Warner came over to Quantico to do the honors in this ceremony. The promotions were held in a private room of the officer's club. My promotion came first with General Warner and Grace pinning my second star on my uniform. Then I was asked to put Colonel Johnson's star on him, with his wife taking her part. All in all, it was a pleasant and yet prestigious ceremony. General Warner shook my hand and congratulating me and then he shook Brigadier General Johnson's hand. General Johnson and his wife both glowed with pride, and rightfully so. After, General Johnson invited Grace and I along with his wife to come to his office for a few minutes.

When we entered the CIE headquarters building. The cheering was almost deafening. These people like General Johnson and I had worked with and got along well with many that were here now. We both saluted them to their surprise. We then went into his office. When we were in his office, he turned and saluted me with a big smile on his face. Then he told me, "I am sure this position and promotion is due to your recommendation and I thank you. From what I know of your history, I will take my slower path for promotions than your promotion rate. How many times have you been shot so far?"

"Well, to tell you the truth, I haven't kept track. But it is a few more times than Grace or I care to remember. The worst time was right here on Quantico. They came close to taking me out that time. And Grace and I had been married only a short time. At times it seems that Grace has spent more time at my side in hospitals than side by side going for walks. This too will pass in time. And good luck to you and keep your head down." With that Grace and I left for our home.

We were settled in this time and it seemed nice enough. Two stars seem to help with some benefits that enlisted or low-ranking officers don't get. The benefits of two stars has something to look forward to, but it is not all peaches and cream. I think the target that seemed to be painted on my back just got much bigger with the second star.

On my days off, I have the chance to show Grace the base and historic sites in the DC area. It is interesting. It is a good place to visit, but not one we like to live in. But this too will pass.

I have finally received permission to look for Colonel Oakley's killers. I can't do this full time but I'm free to work on that for two days a week. I spent some time with Brigadier General Johnson to be filled in on any details from the initial investigation. It wasn't much but it was a start. Colonel Oakley was killed on the base but the culprits were never found. The information concerning them was limited. Colonel Oakley was killed when he went to his vehicle at the end of the day.

Evidently the killers had gotten into his car and ducked down and waited for him to get in. He had either been forced to drive to the location where he was actually tortured and then left for dead or one of the killers drove them to that site.

That was about all that was known about the killing. Dan asked if he could see the clothes the Colonel was wearing at the time? Dan was led to a locked room and taken inside where a locker was opened and the clothes and personal effects were removed for Dan's inspection.

Dan began a detailed inspection. There were only a couple of things Dan found that might be of significance. One was some threads and a small fragment of material caught on the belt buckle of the Colonel's clothes. Dan placed them in an envelope for microscopic examination. Also, there were large blood stains on the clothes on the front and left side of the jacket the Colonel was wearing, and a small blood stain on the right collar. Dan requested a pair of good scissors so he could cut two small pieces of each of the blood stains. After he had the scissors, Dan cut two fragments of each of the blood-stained areas and put them in a pair of separate envelopes.

Dan then asked to see the postmortem report, after the clothes and personal effects were put back into the locker.

Back in Brigadier General Johnson's office the autopsy report was handed to Dan. Dan read the report and asked for a copy of the report. There was something about the report that seemed unusual. He couldn't place what the problem was at the time but by having the report he could look it over again after he had been able think about it and ponder the problem. Dan hoped to figure out what struck him as not correct. The next morning, he realized what the problem with the report was. The conclusion that came to him was that there was not a mistake but rather something was missing. But what he couldn't tell yet.

Dan then took one set of blood-stained cloth fragments to the CIE laboratory for blood type analysis as well as part of the threads and part of the fragment of cloth found caught on the Colonel's belt buckle. He took the other set of samples to the FBI laboratory. He requested a report as soon as any of the tests were complete.

Two days later Dan had the results in his hands from both labs.

The largest blood stain was A+, the blood type of Colonel Oakley. The large blood stain was that of blood lost by him. The small stain was O+. So now we, or I, know the blood type of one of the killers. He is type O+. I had an inquiry to make.

This time the request I had was, "Who on Quantico had type O+ blood?" I went to the records office and made that inquiry. I knew that would require some time so I made a second request, that being to look at the records of individuals who were transferred or retired in the last year. At the time my first request was finished I was nearly through with my search, which I finished about two hours later. The two searches resulted in three names, one still on base, one retired and one transferred.

Now I had a place to start my search for the murderers of Colonel Oakley. I would interview the one still here, Master Sergeant Holmes. The retired individual was a colonel, Irene Ogden. Since the retiree was a female, I am not considering her for the time being. The man that was transferred, Major Watson, had been transferred to Fort Carson. Interesting.

I checked on Sergeant Holmes and found that he was in the hospital as the result of a work-related injury that had occurred four days prior to the murder of Colonel Oakley. He was not released until three days after the murder. And even then, he was in no condition to attempt to murder the Colonel. It looks like I need to return to Fort Carson, for a few days at least.

The results of the examination of the fragment of cloth and the threads were such that if the cloth could be found a positive identification would be possible. But it would have to be the actual piece of clothing used by one of the killers. A long shot but conceivable.

A look at the retired colonel's medical records showed that it was not possible for her to have been physically involved with the murder. She had a small stature and had been sick for a time and was rather weak. Scratch another from the list. The major at Fort Carson was the only candidate left from the list of individuals with blood type O+.

Dan went to General Warner and discussed what he had found to date. He also outlined what he figured he had to do to move the investigation forward to find the murderers of Colonel Oakley. General Warner stated that he needed time to think over the information Dan had given him.

Shortly afterward, Dan received the reports on the threads and fragments of cloth that had been found on Colonel Oakley's belt buckle. The cloth was a special kind of cloth, silk, which was probably from an expensive garment such as a shirt. The threads were also of silk. This implied to Dan that the individual was an egotist and spent his money on self-gratification. One that liked special clothes. What was the major like? A review of his records might produce a mental picture of him.

Dan obtained a copy of the major's records. He was an intelligent officer and usually did a good job. But he tended to put the men down mentally that worked under him He would usually have his uniforms special made of more expensive material. Major Watson seemed to fit the picture all too well.

Dan took this new information to General Warner who asked to discuss this with General Austin. Dan explained the information he had gleaned and then his conclusions. Dan asked for permission to go to Fort Carson and question Major Watson. General Austin thought for a few minutes, asking specific questions every once in a while. When it appeared that he had reached a decision, he told me, "I give you permission to do as you requested as long as you take four CIE personnel with you and request additional body guards from the commander, General Vickers. Is that understood?"

"Yes Sir."

General Warner and I were dismissed and we left. I then went to our quarters at Quantico and talked with Grace. She wasn't happy to see me go and I came up with a plan to send Grace to her family's place while I was at Fort Carson. That went over better. We flew to Denver and I asked Agent McCloud if he could have a couple of agents escort Grace and Helen to Cleaveland.

Agent McCloud's response went something like this,"

Okay, on one condition. That is if you allow me in on the arrest of this major if it turns out that he is one of the guilty parties in the murder of the Colonel. You see, your escapades are far more interesting than the ones we usually encounter."

The agents escorted Grace and Helen to Cleaveland and remained as body guards and Dan headed to Fort Carson. When he came to the main gate, the security officer said that he was not allowed in and Major General Daniel Jorgensen stepped out of the car and put on his coat with two stars on the shoulders. He told the security officer, "With the authority I hold, I out rank your commander, General Vickers. I am now ordering a complete lock down of Fort Carson effective immediately. Now, do you understand me?"

"Yes Sir ".

"Lock the gates and tell all guard posts to lock down tight immediately. This is under the command of Major General Daniel Jorgensen of the CIE and staff member of the Chief of Staff. Shut them down. Now lieutenant, you can tell me where Major Watson can be found."

"Sir he is the Deputy Commander of the Security Forces."

"Get me the Security Forces Commander on the phone immediately."

"I'm sorry Sir, he is on leave at this time."

"Alright, get me General Vickers, the commander of the Rangers Battalion, and the Commander of one of the units of armored infantry, now!"

"Yes Sir."

The first one on the line was General Vickers and Dan told him" I have had the base locked down and I need a Ranger battalion and a couple of companies of armored infantry. They are to seal off the security forces compound and allow no one in or out. This is a matter of national security and if you want to contact General Austin or General Warner you are welcome to do so. But the lock down must happen right now! I am on my way to the security forces headquarters now and if it isn't locked down heads will roll!"

About that time he was informed that Agent McCloud of the FBI was requesting entrance.

"Let him in, but no one else unless Agent McCloud has brought reinforcements ".

Not too long later Agent McCloud was allowed to enter with six FBI vehicles carrying four agents in each. Dan welcomed them and then got in a security police car and took off for the security police headquarters. Upon arrival Dan saw rangers surrounding the building and armored personnel carriers and tanks around the building also.

Dan got out of the car and a colonel and lieutenant colonel came up to him, saluted and the colonel asked him, "What is going on?"

"We are here to make sure one of the most heinous criminals and traitorous officers of the American Army, after Benedict Arnold, is holed up. I want to enter the building with one squad of rangers and the FBI agents. No one is to come out until I give the all clear "

Dan checked his Colt 45 and signaled for the rangers and FBI to accompany him. They entered the main door. Upon entering they encountered some of the security officers with their guns drawn. Dan ordered them to holster their weapons. "In case you haven't noticed I have a battalion of rangers and a couple of companies of armored infantry outside. Anyone who resists will be shot or arrested. Put your guns down."

Just then Major Watson came out with a gun in his hand and ordered his men to arrest me. I told him, "Drop your gun or be shot." He then fired at me three times. Dan fell back but fired and hit the major in the leg. The major fell to the ground and screamed at Dan. The FBI raced forward and subdued the major and handcuffed him.

Dan then told the major, "I arrest you for the murder of Colonel Oakley, conspiracy to commit murder, grand larceny, kidnapping, sale of secret defense information and anything else I can find out about you. I was ordered by the Commander in Chief, President Dwight David Eisenhower to track you down, and I will also track down your murder partner. That is if he doesn't surrender himself for self-preservation." Dan pointed to the captain of the security police and instructed him, "Take this scum away and lock him up. I don't ever want to see him again ".

About that time a female security officer approached him and said, "I'm sorry Sir, but you have been hit." She then told someone to call for an ambulance.

The medical people arrived and took me away. I guess someone lifted the closure of this building. After I had been fixed up in the hospital, General Vickers showed up and said, "You sure do like to make a show of things don't you?"

"Well, I wanted to make absolutely sure Major Watson didn't get away and by bringing a strong show of support, show that no one would get the idea that they could stand against my orders. Like President Teddy Roosevelt said, "Speak softly but carry a big stick ". I chose about the biggest stick I could think of. By the way Sir, will you give my respects and thanks to the companies of armored infantry and the battalion of rangers? They did present an impressive show of force that basically prevented the use of unnecessary force or gun fire. Major Watson, I'm sure, hated me and wanted me dead. Nothing would have stopped him short of killing him or, unless you put him down, and my Colt 45 does an excellent job of that." Dan sent word to General Warner that one of the men that had killed Colonel Oakley is in jail. Put that in the news and his partner will surely give himself up.

Dan was treated at the hospital and kept overnight. His injuries were not serious this time. Irritating but not really bad. He had a flesh wound of his left arm. Fortunately, Grace was not here and could not see and anguish over Dan's injury. She had had enough of that already. The next day he was released.

Dan went to General Vickers' office and reported to him the details of how this action came about. He also informed him of his promotion, appointment to the staff of the Chief of Staff and his orders from the President to find the killers of Colonel

Oakley. That murder was part of a situation that threatened the security of this nation, so this action was of top priority for the Army and myself. Dan again said. "I thank you, General Vickers, for your support and I will personally report this to the Chief of Staff, General Austin. Also, I am sorry and apologize for overriding your orders to not allow me on base. But it was necessary as I'm sure you can appreciate. Once again thanks and good day".

Dan left the General's office and visited the commanders of the companies of armored infantry and rangers and thanked them for their support. "As this action was a top priority and of a national security requirement, your support and your men will result in unit commendations which I will write up for general Austin, our Chief of Staff. He will want a personal report from me which he will get ". Dan then departed and left Fort Carson. Dan stopped at the gate and praised the lieutenant for his actions at following his commanders' orders. The lieutenant smiled and stood a bit taller.

Dan then drove to Cleaveland to pick up his family. But there was no one there. He looked around and found a note. The note said. *"General Jorgensen, we have your wife and daughter as well as your wife's entire family. Drop charges on Major Watson and turn him loose and you will get them back safe and sound. Refuse and we will kill one person every two days until you turn him loose. You don't need to try and contact us, we will know as soon as you turn him loose."*

CHAPTER NINETEEN
Vengeance In Action

I called Agent McCloud and asked him where the agents were that were supposed to be watching my family. He told me that they were on their way back to the office because they were told they were no longer needed.

"And who told them that?"

"They said that you did."

"How long ago was that?"

"About a half an hour ago."

I then informed him that my family and my wife's family were kidnapped and being held hostage. "If I don't turn Major Watson loose they will start killing my family and in-laws".

He replied that he would send several agents out immediately to assist.

"The one statement in the note from the kidnappers, *"You don't need to try and contact us, we will know as soon as you turn him loose."*., is significant. It means their source of information about Major Watson being turned loose, or not, is within the Security Police force at Fort Carson".

I next called the Sheriff and informed him of the situation and asked, "If it were possible, could you have the county sealed off? They haven't had time to leave the county, and if you put out an APB for the arrest of the kidnappers, if they are caught in a road block it could end this kidnapping quickly".

I called General Johnson, commander of the CIE and brought him up to date and asked for his assistance. He said he would get on this immediately.

There wasn't much I could do here in Cleaveland so I headed back to Fort Carson. I needed to talk with General Vickers and the commander of the security police.

Dan was on his way to Fort Carson and as he approaches the county line there was a road block of state police and county deputies. Dan stopped and got out of his car. One of the state policemen drew his hand gun and orders him to stop. Dan did so and one of the deputies approached him and asked, "Who are you?" Dan replied, "Major General Daniel Jorgensen of the US Army CIE and assistant to the Army Chief of Staff. It is my family and the family of my wife that have been kidnapped. And I am the one that requested that the borders of this county be sealed."

"May I see some ID?"

Dan pulled out his wallet and showed the deputy his drivers license and his military ID. The deputy looked at them and then showed them to the state policeman that was holding his gun on Dan. He looked at them and apologized to Dan.

Dan told him, "You were doing the proper thing. It is just that I wanted this procedure finished quickly so I might get to Fort Carson to question the major that I arrested. He is the one that the kidnapping took place in an effort to get him released and an effort to retaliate against me. They have tried to kill me several times and have not succeeded yet. I would say they are getting a bit ticked off at me. And me at them."

One of the state police officers came towards me and said, "Sir, it looks like the net has caught the kidnappers. They are about an hour away from here. Would you like to go there?"

"Would I? You better believe I would. Let's go!"

The road block was cleared, I turned around and one of the state police cars took off, lights flashing and siren screaming, and with me on his tail. That one hour had at least ten minutes cut off. When we arrived, the law enforcement crew stepped back and let me through. Grace was almost in shock. Her father was dead. The other members of the family were alive but disturbed and shocked. Grace ran to me and threw her arms around me and sobbed.

Two of the kidnappers were dead, one wounded and one with no injuries. I ordered him taken to Fort Carson for interrogation. The injured to be taken there to the hospital and taken care of medically and then locked up. I thanked all of the officers for their great assistance. One had been shot but not seriously injured. All were to received commendations, regardless of which roadblock they were involved with.

When all was finished at the site I took my entire family and headed for Cleaveland. A short distance on the road to Cleaveland, Grace's mother asked if they could go to Fort Carson with me. They would feel safer there.

I could find no way to tell Grace and her family, my family, how I felt about what had been done to them because of me. I hoped they had some understanding about that. When I arrived at Fort Carson, the officer at the gate looked at me with a funny expression and told me that I was to go directly to General Vickers' office.

When I arrived there, I asked that my family be allowed to have a room where they could be undisturbed and provided with something to drink.

Then I reported to General Vickers. He was angry. Not necessarily at me, but angry in general. It seemed that Major Watson had escaped. I told him about the note found in the Herndon home and my interpretation of what was said. I told the general, "The implication of the statement, *You don't need to try and contact us, we will know as soon as you turn him loose"*. means that the source of that information could only be from within the Security Force ".

"I want to know what office would have access to such information and who worked in those offices and on which shifts. Also, if Major Watson was assisted in his escape. I want the names of the individuals that could have helped him escape. That means all who could have helped, regardless of shift. Also, with your permission, I don't think it would be a good idea to let anyone in the security forces leave the building and leave the base. The security building should be surrounded again and shut down ".

General Vickers considered Dan's recommendation for a few minutes and then agreed. Then he gave the order. Dan was sure this wouldn't build General Vickers' popularity.

After Dan's meeting with General Vickers, he went to the Security Police headquarters. When he entered, he saw quit a number of angry expressions. The first person he wanted to see was their commander, Colonel Schnell. Colonel Schnell approached him and asked, "What is going on?"

"Let's go into your office. Then we can discuss the situation."

Dan explained about the kidnapping of his family and the note left in the Herndon family home. "The one sentence had critical implications, *You don't need to try and contact us, we will know as soon as you turn him loose.* The indications and my conclusion of those indications that I came up with after reading the note, is that the only way they would know Major Watson was released as soon as it had happened would be if the information came from this building".

Colonel Schnell immediately understood that. The Colonel then told Dan that Major Watson had escaped from the detention area. "I suspect someone here helped him get away."

"How long ago did he escape?"

"About forty-five minutes ago. And I'm afraid that he has left the base."

"Colonel Schnell, here is the information I need. The statement *"we will know as soon as you turn him loose"*. means that the source of that information would be from within the Security Force. I want to know what office would have access to such information and who worked in those offices and on which shifts. Also, Major Watson was assisted in his escape. I want the names of the individuals that could have helped him escape, that means all who could have helped, regardless of shift."

Colonel Schnell thought for a moment and then said, "I think we can have that information in about fifteen minutes."

"Great. That will help considerably."

Dan went out into the foyer and observed the people. From the looks on their faces, he wouldn't have much of a chance in a popularity poll or in front of a firing squad. No one approached him and no one spoke to him. The fact that Dan had two stars on his shoulders and wore a CIE insignia probably prevented any verbal or physical response from this belligerent group of people. If only they knew, but they would know shortly.

A short time later Colonel Schnell approached Dan and handed him a sheet of paper. They went back into the colonel's office. Dan did a quick survey of the lists of names. Dan then asked Colonel Schnell, "How long has Major Watson been at Fort Carson and how long he has he been your deputy?"

"He has been at Fort Carson about four months and he was made deputy as soon as he got to the base."

Dan thought about this information for a few seconds and asked the colonel for his impressions of the major. "Major Watson was a competent officer and deputy. But it seemed that he had a constant chip on his shoulders. My impression is that he figured that he was smarter than anyone else and that he should be the commander. He also looked like he was a woman's man. I believe he figured that he was god's gift to the ladies."

That answered several of Dan's questions. There were not many women's names on the lists he held in his hand. Two names showed up on both lists, both women. A lieutenant Harris and Airman First Class Fletcher. Dan pointed this out to Colonel Schnell and asked for both women, if they were still in the building, to be taken to detention rooms.

A few minutes later, a captain reported to the colonel and Dan. "Sir, we have Airman Fletcher in one of out detention rooms, but Lieutenant Harris is not in the building. She is supposed to be here but is not."

Dan ordered, "Put out an All-Points Bulletin (APB) for the lieutenant and she is to be arrested. She is to be considered as armed and dangerous."

Dan then had the captain take him to where the airman

was being held and asked the captain to be with him all during the interrogation. Dan also requested for a stenographer to be present. She arrived within two minutes and the captain led them into the room.

Airman Fletcher was frightened and her appearance showed an increase in her anxiety when she saw me. I asked her some general questions which seemed to ease her fear level a bit. Then I asked her, "What was your impression of Major Watson?" With that question her face made an immediate change from fear to anger and repulsion. Her answer had a bitter tone and she said, "He was an egotistical ass. He acted like he expected every woman to fall on her knees and kiss his feet. And he treated us as simpering little children. I hope he gets shot so he can't come back here." Her response seemed to be genuine and without forethought. I believed her.

I then asked her of her impressions of Lieutenant Harris. Her response wasn't too much different from that of her feelings towards the major. A very hard and angry look came onto her face and her entire body. She said, "That bitch could see no one other than the major. She fawned all over him and would do anything for him."

"Could she have called out any information about the major or helped him to escape?"

"In a heartbeat. Is that what this is all about?"

"Yes. Is there a record of phone calls she may have made over the last 24 to 36 hours?"

The captain said, "Yes Sir. That information could be supplied in about five minutes."

I thanked Airman Fletcher for her cooperation and help and that she was being released. I did ask her to remain in the building in case I thought of any other question that she might be able to answer.

She got a big smile on her face and thanked me. She did something that was not quite according to military protocol, she threw her arms about me and kissed me.

She stepped back and blushed beautifully. "Sorry Sir." She then departed the room. I turned and saw the captain grinning.

Captain Jonas, the one that had been helping me, came to me about ten minutes later and handed me a list of calls Lieutenant Harris had made over the last thirty-six hours. There were seven calls made. Three were to one number. I asked for the determination of who was at that number. The captain left to obtain that information He returned a few minutes later. "The person at that number and at the times the calls were made, was a Sergeant Monroe of the Colorado Springs Police Department."

I asked that he be held for questioning. Captain Jonas told me, "That order has already been made. I was told that Sergeant Monroe had left the building for reasons unknown. I have requested an "All-Points Bulletin" be put out immediately for his arrest with the warning that he was armed and dangerous."

This situation was becoming more complicated. But if they could get hold of one end of one of the strings, that may lead to all of the others. That, at least was Dan's hope.

Dan went to Colonel Schnell and told him the findings thus far and asked for his permission to speak to his people that were still being held in the building. They need and deserve to know the truth as I know it and hoped it to be the real truth.

The Colonel and Dan went out into the foyer and the Colonel asked for everyone that could to come to the foyer. This took a few minutes amid a dull buzz of whispered conversation. When they were together, the colonel called them to attention and they all snapped to attention. Dan then stepped forward and told them, "At ease. I want to thank all of you for your patience and help. I also want to apologize for having to basically hold you as prisoners in your own building, but the situation was dangerous and I wished to contain that danger. Unfortunately, those actions were a bit late. But we are now on the track of the people that were probably responsible. Major Watson is wanted for the torture and murder of Colonel Oakley, CIE commander, and for treason, just so you know why I was acting with so much control over the expected situation. Once again, my apologies and my grateful appreciation for your dedication and efforts.

Believe me, there will be a unit award and some personal awards for the actions of this unit and all members this day."

Dan was no longer looked at as if he were the enemy. Several people came forward and requested an opportunity to speak with General Jorgensen. The captain made arrangements for each to have that opportunity. Dan requested for a stenographer to be present and asked Captain Jonas to be present when a female was being interviewed. The interviews added pertinent information that would help if the major were ever to be brought to trial. The captain and Colonel Schnell also gave interviews. They had some needed information that would help when the time came.

Word came a couple of hours later, that the lieutenant and Sergeant Monroe had been rounded up, but the lieutenant had resisted arrest and had been wounded. She was in critical condition and not expected to live. The sergeant was being difficult but his fellow policemen were confident that given time, he would answer their questions.

Dan didn't expect any answers from the lieutenant, even if she were in condition to talk. The sergeant was the one he wanted to question now. He went to the city jail and requested permission to question him and for a stenographer to be present. The Chief of Police agreed on the condition that he could be present and ask a few questions himself to which Dan had no problem.

They entered the holding cell and they all introduced themselves. The Chief of Police began the questioning. The sergeant would not answer. Dan began with his questions. Again, no answer. Dan then began by telling him the federal charges against him. Dan said, "I will personally see you charged with murder, conspiracy to commit murder, kidnapping, grand larceny, charges of spying and sale of secret information and a few more charges when I am finished checking out the files we have against you. Even with the chances of appeals, you won't live five to seven years because there are those in prison that will know about you and be willing to cut your throat. And every day for every year you will die a thousand times. It will finally come to the point where you will greet death as an old friend. You are like the person Shakespeare wrote about when he wrote, *A coward dies a thousand times before his death, but the valiant taste of death but once.* You will see your death many times the thousand. There is only one way you can avoid those thousand deaths. Tell us now what you know and you might avoid those deaths. Goodbye, coward ".

Dan and the Police Chief arose and began to leave, along with the stenographer. They were nearly all out of the cell when the sergeant called for them to come back. After they were settled, the sergeant began to talk. The confessions he gave and the supporting information were enough to put the major and a few others behind bars for years or put their necks in nooses. When he finished I asked the stenographer to transcribe and type the statement and then we will have him sign it. The Chief and I will witness this statement. The Chief nodded his head with a look on his face and in his eyes that would cause a person to cower.

We left the holding cell and I asked the Chief, "Do you want to hold him or shall we transfer him to Fort Carson or let the Feds have him?" The Chief thought about that and then said, "Take him to Fort Carson. I don't want to see him again."

When the transcript of the statement was finished, Dan and the Chief took it in to the Sergeant for his signature. Dan and the Chief then signed it as witnesses. The stenographer had signed it earlier.

Dan then took the statement; had it copied photographically and took a copy to the prosecutor of the Department of justice in Denver. The prosecutor would determine charges which could be filed and which suspects to arrest. When that list was finished, Dan and the FBI would be busy again rounding up all of the suspects if possible. If Dan's memory were correct, there must have been twenty to twenty-five people the security forces of Fort Carson and Peterson Field would have to pick up.

Two days later they had a list of suspects to round up. The roundup was scheduled for two days later. Eight were on Fort Carson and six others on Peterson Field.

On the scheduled day, Dan got the Fort Carson Security

Police team together and gave them their assignments with instructions to move out in twenty minutes, under the supervision of Colonel Schnell. Dan then went to Peterson Field and met with the Wing Commander, Colonel Wardell and Lieutenant Colonel Jameson, Commander of the Security Force. Dan reminded them of what was happening and gave the Lieutenant Colonel the list of people to be picked up on the base. He just about collapsed when he saw the list. Colonel Wardell snatched the list from the Lieutenant Colonel's hand. His face blanched when he saw the list of names. The Colonel asked, "Are you sure? "

"Yes."

Included on the list was the name of one member of the security force and three individuals in critical positions on base. One name on the list, which Dan questioned, was Senior Airman Fletcher. Dan did not want to take action in this roundup. Airman Fletcher's name on the list had deflated Dan as well when he first saw her name on the list.

A couple of hours later, Dan called Agent McCloud and asked for a report on how their roundup activities fared. They had captured forty six of forty-seven suspects. Dan told him that the five suspects on Fort Carson and the three suspects on Peterson Field had been captured.

All in all, sixty of sixty-one suspects had been arrested. Dan didn't feel entirely good about this activity. He wondered if Airman Fletcher were actually guilty. That had not been his impression, and his impressions were usually accurate. The individuals doing the investigations, hopefully would determine the truth. And if his impression were correct, the investigations would prove her innocence. Drag nets often captured the good and the bad and then it was necessary to separate the two. But would that be the actual result if he stayed out of this situation?

Dan needed to go back and read the statement of Sergeant Monroe again. To see what he had to say about Airman Fletcher. When Dan went through the statement, there was no mention of Airman Fletcher at all. This raised a big, red flag in Dan's head about the Federal Prosecutor. Dan went over the statement with a fine-tooth comb, making a list of all of the people mentioned in that document. Then he compared it with the list from the prosecutor. There were fifty-seven names in the statement. Of those, only forty-four were listed to be arrested. There were sixty-one on the arrest list. That meant that sixteen that should not have been arrested were, and thirteen that should have been arrested were not. This stunk to high heaven.

Of the seventeen that should have been arrested but were not, four were from Fort Carson and two were from Peterson Field. Dan got on the phone to Colonel Schnell and reported his findings and requested that the four not arrested were to be picked up. I read off the four from Fort Carson and added that it was imperative that they be picked up immediately. He agreed and would carry that out now.

Dan then called Lieutenant Colonel Jameson and repeated the same message to him. I read off the two names of individuals not arrested and asked that they be picked up without delay.

I then called Agent McCloud and told him the same information. Six individuals that should have been arrested but were not, four were from Fort Carson and two from Peterson Field. Those six individuals were in the process at this time of being picked up by Army or Air Force security officers.

I then read off the eleven that were not on Fort Carson or Peterson Field and had not been arrested. The eleven should have been arrested and Dan requested they be picked up ASAP.

I also requested that we, Agent McCloud and myself, go to the federal prosecutor's office and question him immediately. And if he were responsible for the arrest list, arrest him. Unless he had legitimate reasons to arrest those not named in the statement. If the person responsible were someone else, then arrest whomever immediately. This was to be done while the seventeen suspects were being picked up by federal or military personnel.

We went to the Federal Prosecutor's office and questioned him. He was totally unable, or unwilling, to explain any of the differences between the two lists. The lists being, first the names from the confession and statement of Sergeant Monroe, that should have been arrested. The second list of names put together by the Federal Prosecutor and indicated these individuals were to be arrested. The response by the prosecutor left no alternatives for Agent McCloud or Dan but to arrest him.

This roundup was completed within three hours. Those arrested included the federal prosecutor. The individuals arrested but not on Dan's arrest list, which Dan extracted from Sergeant Monroe's confession and statement, and should not have been arrested, were to be interviewed. After their interviews, if the information available supported the individual's answers, then they were to be released.

The people to be interviewed, from Peterson Field included Airman Fletcher. Dan interviewed her again to determine if she were guilty or not. She was very nervous during the interview. Her answers were those of a person that didn't know what was going on and her reactions were not those with a formerly thought up story. She acted and answered like a person not guilty and didn't answer with made up information. When he was finished, he told her how she had been arrested in the first place and Dan was releasing her and removing any mention of this incident from her records. She brightened up and said, "Thank you." She was allowed to leave. Dan then recommended that she be given a one week leave as compensation and for recuperation.

Agent McCloud was able to arrest those that should have been arrested and released those that weren't supposed to be arrested. Major Watson was still at large. As was the major's partner in the murder of Colonel Oakley. Agent McCloud had the major listed on the ten most wanted. How long would the major be able to avoid capture?

A few days later, Dan and his wife were in town when they walked across the parking lot at a store Grace wanted to visit. Suddenly there were some shots and Dan fell to the ground. The shooter came around a truck and approached Dan, with his gun pointed at Dan to finish him off. When he got close Grace, who had pulled out her 38 when the shooting started, opened fire at close range. She put three rounds through the killer's forehead. He was dead before he hit the ground. In a couple of minutes, the police arrived and an ambulance. They rushed up to Dan. Dan was trying to sit up, his body amour had saved his life again.

The man that attempted to kill Dan was none other than Major Watson. **How many times had this man died before he died under fire from a protective wife and mother, It isn't wise to anger a woman.** The major had never even looked at Grace, a fatal mistake.

Grace and Dan both hoped that they now could live in peace for ever after. Dan and Grace have spent three months recovering from the shooting of the major. A report of his death had gone out to the news agencies where everyone had a chance to read it. And the next result happened just as Dan had predicted. The murder partner of Major Watson gave himself up. Dan's obligation was complete. What to do now? With no lists with an agenda that demanded Dan's time, They spent a couple of weeks considering the pros and cons of going back to Knoxville College to teach. Their conclusion was to go back.

EPILOGUE

Dan and his family went to Knoxville and visited with the County Sheriff who was elated to see Dan, Grace and Helen. They had a pleasant visit before Dan asked the Sheriff, "Have the people of Knoxville and President Wilson recovered from their hatred of me? Do you think they would accept us if I were to come back here and teach at the college?"

The Sheriff beamed at the mention of Dan coming back to Knoxville and said, "I hope you come back. I would enjoy having you here, even if no one else would. President Wilson seems to regret how he treated you before and I think he would be glad to have you at the school again ".

Dan and his family then went to the college to talk with President Wilson. The President's receptionist quickly ushered Dan and family into the President's office with an introduction. President Wilson heartedly welcomed them and offered them seats. After some small talk he asked Dan, "Will you please come back and teach? You affected your students like no other teacher ever did that I had ever seen and observed. You could have the same home you had before, and teach biology, martial arts and ROTC". President Wilson again begged Dan to come back.

Finally, Dan informed President Wilson of their decision to return and teach. He was happy with Dan's decision, and said, "The board of governors will be pleased and I just might be able to keep my job."

They moved into the home that was so pleasant and welcoming. Dan and Grace felt at home. Grace's mother sold their home in Cleaveland and moved to Knoxville to be close to Grace and Helen.

With Dan and his family, Grace's family along with a few students that were members of the church, there were enough members in Knoxville to form a branch of the Church. This made it possible to have church services in Knoxville. Dan was called as branch president. They could have church meetings here, which was good for the family.

Dan was able to reach an agreement with President Wilson and the Board of Directors to rent classrooms at the college where Church meetings could be held. This would provide a financial advantage for the college as well as space for the church activities.

It was great that Grace's mother and family were now living nearby, especially good now that Grace was pregnant again. Grace was hoping for a boy this time. Time would tell.

www.ingramcontent.com/pod-product-compliance
Lightning Source LLC
LaVergne TN
LVHW021817060526
838201LV00058B/3425